W, Fict

14537p

AN EVANS NOVEL OF THE WEST

HORSE THIEVES

NELSON NYE

M. EVANS & COMPANY, INC. NEW YORK

For That Great Sleuth of
Extraneous Facts
JOHN DOUGLAS GILCHRIESE

Library of Congress Cataloging-in-Publication Data

Nye, Nelson C. (Nelson Coral), 1907–
    Horse thieves / Nelson Nye.
        p.   cm. — (An Evans novel of the West)
    ISBN 0-87131-518-1
    I. Title.   II. Series
    PS3527.Y33H6   1987
    813'.54—dc19   87-15345 CIP

M. Evans and Company, Inc.
216 East 49 Street
New York, New York 10017

Manufactured in the United States of America

9 8 7 6 5 4 3 2 1

Chapter One

First time I laid eyes on Merrilee Manton was on a mighty dark night. She was in the front room of her house at Rafter bending over some sort of low table with a towel bunched up on it; I could see that much in the reflected light from the room beyond. She heard my step through the half-opened outside door. As I came onto the porch, she spun round, straightening, with a gun in her fist.

"I've a damn good mind to put a bullet in you!"

"I called out twice while I was still in the saddle. Gettin' no answer I was fixing to knock—"

"Think you'll know me next time we meet?"

"Wouldn't bet on it, ma'am. Expect you'll look some different with clothes on."

"Stop gawping, and get off that porch before I let you have it!"

She had that gun pointed square at my brisket, so I reckoned the smartest thing I could do was get off it, which I did. I went and stood by my sorrel gelding, taking long breaths, trying to get my pulse back to normal. She had platinum hair, cut short and kind of wavy, but how she looked between that and her shoulders I couldn't have told for all the gold in the bank at Buda. What she had below was about as good as they come and was bright in my mind when she came out of the house tucking the tails of a shirt into blue denim pants. "What were you looking for out on that porch?"

A pair of kids caught in the hay would have looked more flustered than she did right then. She had all her priorities in the right place and hadn't even bothered to fetch out her gun.

"I already told you. I went up there to knock."

"Then suppose you explain how you happened to be here."

"They told me in Peña Blanca you might be in need of a wrangler."

"Peña Blanca," she said dryly, "will never be mistaken for the hub of the universe. What were you doing there?"

It wasn't easy to think with those brown eyes so coolly skewering me. What she had between hair and shoulders was every bit as good as what she had below them. A real looker!

"Well," I said, fiddlin' with my horse like I figured he was getting restless, "they told me in Tombstone I might find a job here."

"Who told you?"

"One of them Crystal Palace barkeeps."

That got me a long hard look. She said, "You sound like a Texican. Somebody chase you out of there?"

"Not exactly, ma'am. Thought Arizona might be better for my health."

She considered me some more. "You don't look very puny. What were you doing where you came from?"

"Wind Rock, ma'am. I got my start wrangling horses."

"If you want a job here quit backing and filling."

"If you got to know, ma'am, I had a little misunderstandin'. You see, I had this job as a deputy and being sort of undersized for that part of the country—five foot eight to be

2

exact—it become a kind of survival habit to get my iron out first in any ruckus. It didn't rightly make me a heap of friends. Folks got to calling me a so-and-so gunslinger, which I ain't—"

"I'll take your word for it," she said with a touch of impatience. "What do I call you?"

"Peep Boyano."

"What does a wrangler do, Boyano?"

"Wrangles . . . that's what *we* always did."

That sharp look was back in the way she was eyeing me. "In regard to horses—*caballos* to you."

"I can perform in either language, ma'am."

"And for heaven sakes, stop ma'aming me. My name's Merrilee Manton. Now quit sidetracking this conversation and tell me what a wrangler is expected to do."

"Well, horse wranglin', Miz Manton, ma'am, is generally given to a boy or green hand. The day wrangler—leastways over around Wind Rock where I come from, is called a wrangatang. Fellow that has the night job is the night hawk. We say he's swapped his bed for a lantern. His job's to keep the saddle stock from straying where it's unhandy to catch them. On a roundup when the camp has to be moved it's the night hawk's duty to drive the hoodlum wagon. Where I got my schoolin' a wrangler was known as the remudero. He had charge of the remuda. Likewise a wrangler has to help the cook gather stuff for his fire and get his teams hooked up. He's expected to keep the remuda on good grass—"

"All right, I guess you've been there. On a horse ranch we do things a mite different. All hands are wranglers, and the foreman decides which hand does what and when. Rafter's foreman is Stovepipe Johnson, not the easiest man you'll come across to get along with. Do what you're told, and he'll have no complaint."

It was too dark in the yard to see very much. "You're hirin' me?"

"What you came for, wasn't it?"

"That's right."

I watched her glance saunter over me again. "A gentleman," she said, "would have respected a lady's privacy."

"Lordy, ma'am, I ain't no gentleman. Just an orphaned half-Mex whose mama took off after she got me delivered . . . couldn't stand the chili, I expect, or all them gymnastics everyday and every night."

She considered that, and me along with it. I thought to catch a glint of amusement, but if I had it was gone like wind hustling over a field of wheat. "Anyway," I said, "I didn't know you was private when I stepped on your porch."

"That's enough on that subject."

"These horses," I said, "were they bred on this place?"

"Some were. Some were collected by my father during his travels before settling down at this tag end of nowhere."

"Pretty valuable, are they?"

She skewered me again with that cool direct stare. "If you hope to get along in this outfit you'd better keep that lip buttoned." Which was when her crew came pounding into the yard in a great swirl of dust. While they still sat on their horses looking me over, she said, short and crisp, "This is Peep Boyano, boys, latest addition to the Rafter work force," and went into the house.

Chapter Two

There were seven of us followed the top screw of this outfit, Stovepipe Johnson, over to the one empty corral where, after unsaddling, we left our mounts and trooped along back of him across to the bunkhouse. This was built of adobe, about forty feet long and maybe twenty feet wide. With the Rochester lamp lit above the long table with its bolted-down benches, we stood a few moments taking stock of each other.

Johnson looked at me longest, a sandy-haired man with rope-scarred fists and plenty of size from his boot heels up. With lips cracked apart in a lazy grin he said, "There'll be no pranks," and I hadn't no doubt he meant every word of it. He didn't look to be a man whose authority was questioned. He showed me which bunk he wanted me in, and after telling Skeeter Jones what he expected for breakfast, the lamp was put out and we all turned in.

Before I joined the chorus of snores it crossed my mind this was a pretty large crew for an outfit devoted to nothing but horses. But mostly I thought about Merrilee Manton.

After grub next morning and the crew put to work at various chores, Johnson said, "Come along and I'll show you round. Old man came out of Texas with half the horses you'll see here now. Had the whole place fenced with chain link—hate to think what it cost him. Three hundred and fifty acres. Dug six wells an' put windmills on 'em. Likewise fenced, we've sixty acres of planted grass divided into pastures."

After eyeing a few of the equine tenants I didn't hardly know what to think of this place. At Wind Rock we'd have called these gamblers' horses, Steeldusts and Travelers I'd have said by the looks. "What's she figurin' to do with them?" I asked.

"Sell 'em, I reckon, if she can get her price."

"How many are there?"

"Never stopped to count—around sixty, anyway. I helped him collect the ones we fetched out of Texas. Couple of studs and twenty mares used strictly for breeding. Rest we raised here."

"How many's she sold?"

"Ain't sold none up to now. Nobody round these parts can afford 'em."

"With the whole place fenced I'd think three hands would be all you'd need."

"We've got four men ridin' fence day and night."

"You had trouble with it?"

"Nothing this crew wasn't able to handle. There's signs out up every five hundred yards warnin' folks away from it. Seems like some around here ain't able to read—we're takin' care of that."

"Polo ponies and brush track sprinters. Must be worth real money."

"The two studs are sons of Traveler out of old Billy mares. The twenty mares we been breedin' have damn good pedigrees. If you come out of Texas I expect you've heard of Judge Welch, Texas Chief, Little Joe, and some of them others, all sons of Traveler. One of them, raised by the Shelys at Alfred, was called King. Man over near Bonita swapped one hundred head of damn good range horses for him and changed his name to Possum. Uncle Mabry Gardner's got another son of Traveler he calls Blue Eyes."

"Yeah. Running fools," I said. "Still, if she can't find a market—unless her old man was in the top brackets—she must be feelin' the pinch."

"He wasn't what you'd call rich. Fencin' these acres took about all he had left. He died three years ago."

"How long had he been here?"

"We came here five years ago. Last year Merrilee had to take out a loan from the Beach and Bascomb bank," Johnson said.

"If she can't find a market, what are you figurin' to do?"

"You'll probably find out if you're here long enough."

I looked at him more careful. With his chin-strapped hat, those batwing chaps, and hung-open vest, his weather-roughened face and rope-scarred hands, smiling through the clamp of tobacco-stained teeth, he had the look of a man who'd been around. He must have read my mind.

"I've heard the owl hoot once or twice. I'm goin' to give you some advice. You been hired to wrangle horses, not to wrangle *with* them. Miz Merrilee don't want their mouths spoiled; I've got strict orders the crew's not to ride 'em. Those old enough to be handled she's broke to the saddle herself. Any hand caught aboard one is discharged on sight. Keep that in mind."

"What am I supposed to be doing?"

"You can make sure the pasture fences ain't breeched."

He'd given me plenty to think about. If the crew had nothing to do with these horses, it seemed like eight hands, counting Johnson and myself, were a lot more than needed. I couldn't see any point to it. From what I had gathered they'd been bothered with occasional would-be horse thieves, so that keeping four hands riding fence wasn't unreasonable in view of the kind of stock being guarded. A foreman and four hands looked to me to be ample.

Eight days on this spread just touring the pastures got to be pretty boring.

On the ninth day Gil Plaza was put on that job, and I was told by Johnson I was wanted up at the house.

I was considerable set up at the thought of chatting with Merrilee again. I even took the time to shave before going over there and knocking on the door. She led me into her office and told me to take a chair "We'll wait for Johnson," she said, leaning against the edge of her desk.

I got the impression she was worried about something.

When Johnson came in with Red Durphy she lost no time getting down to brass tacks. "Last year I took a sizable loan from the Beach and Bascomb bank at Tucson. A simple matter of necessity to keep this place going. I've kept the interest paid but now the first installment against the bank's outlay is due. It's a week past due and I'm not able to pay it."

Johnson said, "They'll probably give you a little time."

"I wish I could think so, but it doesn't seem very likely."

"What did you put up to secure this loan?" asked Durphy, a stocky galoot about five foot nine with a brawler's shoulders, log-fingered hands, and rock-gray eyes in an expressionless face. "You put up the ranch?"

"The ranch and everything on it."

"Including the horses?" I said, and she nodded.

"Naturally I'd no intention of throwing in the horses. They wouldn't make me the loan unless the horses were included. Last week I got a letter from Phil Sneed, the bank's executive officer, reminding me the first installment's due."

"Ten thousand dollars?" Johnson rasped at his jaw.

"Yes—it's a short note. I haven't even got five, let alone ten."

"Guess we'll have to sell somethin'," Johnson mumbled.

"I could probably get that much for Rafter, but we haven't got the time, and I've nothing else to sell." She didn't sound as dispirited as you'd reckon she might.

Red Durphy said, "Guess you'll have to sell some of them bangtails."

Indignation brightened her stare. "Not for what I could get around here!"

"Well," I said, "what are you going to do?"

"He's given me till the fifteenth. After that he says he has no choice but to foreclose. He—"

Horse hoofs and the sound of a buggy came to a stop in front of the porch. Johnson, looking out, said, "That's him now."

"How many days we got left?" Durphy asked as Johnson went off to let in the banker.

"Six," she said, and before we could think of any answers to that Johnson fetched the banker into the room.

"Well," he said, with beady little eyes flashing round like a ferret's, "am I interrupting something?"

"Not really. Mr. Sneed, this is Mr. Boyano. From Texas. He's proposing to buy the Rafter horses. We've just been dis—"

"I'm afraid these horses aren't for sale," the banker said, looking down his nose and ignoring the introduction. "Unless your note is paid in six days those horses—the whole of this property—will belong to Beach and Bascomb. If he still wants the horses he'll have to deal with us."

"What price will you put on them, Snide?"

"The name," he said, inflating his chest like a pouter pigeon, "is Sneed." He looked at me like I was something he'd stepped in. "I doubt if you've got that kind of money—"

"I'm repping for a syndicate," I told him. "For these kinds of horses we're prepared to pay a substantial sum."

"Miss Manton has six more days to pay the first installment on the bank's loan. After that, if she can't meet her obligations we intend to start foreclosure proceedings. Any time after the fifteenth you can come when it suits you and buy what you please. Cash on the barrelhead."

Turning then with a smug satisfaction to run those beady bright eyes over Merrilee again he said, "Sorry to have to leave in such a hurry but I've four more appointments to see to. You've had a year's grace with nothing to pay but the interest—not what we'd do for all of our customers, I assure you. You've six more days to pay that first installment against the principle. If I don't hear from you I'll be back on the seventh with the sheriff to take possession."

Bankers as a breed I'd never had much use for, but I'd been rubbed wrong by that one from the time I'd first laid eyes on him. I thought to myself he was lucky I hadn't hit him.

Merrilee was giving me a rather searching look, which she now turned into a brief but approving smile plainly seen by Red Durphy without the least sign of enthusiasm.

Stovepipe Johnson said, "Reckon we can all see the writin' on the wall. That crocodile's visit didn't leave much to chew on."

"Tomorrow," Merrilee said, "lock, stock, and barrel, we'll be on our way to Goldfield."

Chapter Three

Hard to tell about Johnson, but Durphy and I were so taken by surprise we stood there like a pair of prize fools with our mouths hanging open.

"Don't be such ninnies," she said. "You think I didn't see this coming? They knew I couldn't repay that loan."

"If they knew that much they'll be expectin' you to bolt," Durphy said. "They'll be watchin' this place like hawks!"

"In a couple days, perhaps, when Sneed gets back. By a friendly miracle I might have been able to pay him today. I've been squirreling away supplies for a couple of months; we'll use pack horses out of the remuda. We're leaving nothing but the ranch, and we're not coming back."

"Some of this outfit may plain up an' quit," Durphy growled.

Johnson showed a thin edge of his weather-bitten grin. "Not without they're lookin' to git buried."

"Beach and Bascomb will have the sheriff on our trail quick as they find out we've dug for the tules," Durphy said.

"But with luck that won't be for several days," she reminded him. "I'm not going to trade that stock for any mortgage, you can make up your mind to that."

I said, "You know what happens to horse thieves around here?"

"First they have to catch them. And we're not going to be caught," she replied.

Johnson had been watching us, considering things that weren't yet apparent to me. "You boys have to realize we can't let anyone go and tip them off. No matter what happens we're all in this together."

"But Goldfield!" Durphy growled. "D'you savvy how far away that is?"

"What's a few hundred miles to reach a market like that? The place is booming—has been for months. There's more money in that place than in Tucson, El Paso, and Frisco put together," Merrilee said. "We'll be on our way before sunup tomorrow. Now let's get busy."

Perhaps her decision to turn this outfit into horse thieves was somewhat easier for me to understand than for the rest of the crew; I had a better idea what those animals were worth if she could find the right buyers. In Nevada horses of that caliber were scarcer than hen's teeth. No telling how much some of those boys would shell out.

The pack string was loaded and our outfit on the way well before daylight, heading west to start with. Goldfield was a long way north of us but first we were bound to leave a plain track, and when the posse took after us we'd be a heap better off if the law had no notion of where we were bound for. This would take a bit longer, and we'd have to avoid towns and people who worked on ranches if we could. Some way we had to manage to completely disappear and preferably without a trace.

It wasn't going to be easy. I could see that straightaway. Once you embark on a criminal activity you're invariably faced with more crimes to cover it. Yet I couldn't honestly blame her. I guessed in her boots I'd have done the same. Caught in a bind, the only possible way out—and it wasn't what you'd call any salubrious prospect—was the escape she had chosen. And against this, egged on by the bank, the law was bound to use all its resources, including Indian trackers.

I shook my head more than once considering this. And the penalty if caught, at least for the men swept up in this with her, was hanging.

We made pretty good time that first day but this ducking and dodging was all extra mileage. She rode point with Johnson; I brought up the drag, constantly alert, not only to make sure no horses were lost but with a weather eye out to spot pursuit before it bore down on us or set up an ambush.

All in all a rather trying day for all hands. At noon we lunched on jerky without bothering to stop. We were into the desert by this time, and the sun bore down hot enough to fry an egg anyplace—if you had one.

By midafternoon we were picking our way through several miles of malapais, hotter than the hinges and a first-rate place in all that lava rock for a horse to break a leg at the first sign of carelessness. Getting through this batch slowed us down considerably; the only good thing about it was the possibility of slowing any pursuit even more. And by the time the law took out after us—if providence allowed us the full six days, or even five—on the sandy stretches, if we got a good enough wind our trail mightn't be too easily hung onto.

It was something to hope for anyway.

We stopped in the late afternoon for Gil Plaza, our Spanish cook, to fix us up a bit of canned grub. By that time most of us were hungry enough to eat anything so long as we'd something to wash it down with.

And that was another worry that rode with us, the likely probability of running out of water.

Once we'd filled our bellies and the horse had been fed and cautiously watered, Merrilee insisted on pressing on.

Red Durphy, never shy about his notions, protested. "You'll run these horses ragged," he growled.

"Better to run them ragged than to lose them," she said grimly.

As night came down, that vaguely luminous half-dark of the desert, we got out of that damned black rock and into a region of low, rounded hills. These were bare for the most part, though a few showed brush along their sides. This was easier going—the underfoot part—though keeping track of our charges was made a great deal more difficult. Especially for me, expected to make sure we didn't lose any.

About two hours before dawn we set up camp in a motte of old cottonwoods beside a spring which allowed us to refill our water bags and gave us a chance for cautiously watering the stock. This early in our flight no one suggested any posting of sentries; we just stretched out wherever the fancy struck us.

Before seven o'clock after a rather puny breakfast we were on our way again. Twice coming through that malapais we had changed direction and were now pointed north. At a guess, we were making around nine miles an hour as an average.

We were lucky to have gotten through that lava stretch with all the horses still intact. Though I thought it plain by the twists and turns they were taking, Merrilee and Johnson were hoping to locate either a malapais or a creek with running water to help hide our trail.

By eleven that morning we were back into a broad stretch of desert that appeared to stretch ahead some twenty or thirty miles; in this kind of heat it was a little hard to guess. Regardless of the stinging grit it might lift, all of us, I think, were hoping for a wind, even rain, anything that might help to discourage pursuit.

But what little breeze we got wasn't stiff enough to move

any sand, and not a cloud marred the intense glare of that brassy sky. Soaked with sweat we pushed on. We skipped a noon stop and chewed more jerky, and that evening, in whatever meager shade we could find among the scrub along a dry wash, we stopped long enough for Plaza to cook up a mess of *frijoles y chili*, a pretty popular dish with folks south of the border. It must have reminded Durphy of something he'd been shoving around behind those sun-squinted eyes, for he said of a sudden, "Why didn't we take these horses into Mexico? We could have saved a lot of miles, a heap of wear and tear, and no sheriff could get at us."

Merrilee gave him one of those straight looks of hers. "Not enough *ricos* and too many bandits. And everybody would have their hands out."

That night we slept straight through, those that weren't on night herd. All of us took a whack at that in rotation. Johnson got up last, him being the oldest, easily into his forties, but tough as whang leather. Short watches these were. He roused Plaza out at five, and the rest of us at around quarter past when the half-cooked food was ready.

We got away by six-thirty. A couple hours later we were into another patch of volcanic rock, which we crossed with extreme care, several times switching to the right and left to make our course, if a posse hung onto it, a lot harder to determine.

It was gruelling work, arduous and dangerous to our charges, and more than one curse flared up before we finally got out of it with one horse less than we'd entered it. To look at Merrilee's face you might have thought she'd lost a close relation. But with a broken leg there was nothing to be done but shoot it. And this meant leaving it right where it fell.

We cut east a while then.

Just as we got out of this devil's playground we swung west again. "Headin' for the Colorado," Durphy opined. "If we don't stray too far it will assure us of water and take us straight north into Nevada. Up around Searchlight someplace we'll have to leave it and strike west by north across sage flats and pure damn desert." He looked at me with a derisive grin. "From where we are right now it's still some five hundred miles to Goldfield, an' over the kinda country no one'd hunt for a picnic."

Johnson, Merilee's *segundo*, pulled up by us then.

"Hate to have you boys makin' any brash moves," he said for openers, with a hard roving eye examining us singly and collectively for a handful of moments, finally settling on Red. "You know, Durph, in some circumstances a case of simple homesickness can turn more disastrous than typhoid fever." Allowing this time to sink in while that bright probing glance washed over us again, he said, soft as snake tracks, "Any blatherskite seen about to slip away prob'ly won't have no idea what struck him."

With a knowledgeable nod he went off whistling.

Red Durphy and I exchanged darkening glances, Joe Lucie and Dirk Horba peering bovinely after the nonchalant shape of the broad-backed foreman. No one put their thoughts into words.

With a red blaze of sun sinking behind western hills and turning them into chunks of black cardboard, Johnson, up ahead, sent his voice back to say the horses needed rest so we'd be staying in this trough for the next ten-twelve hours.

We were all glad enough to get down and shake loose a few cramps, I reckoned. This was the end of a long fourth day, and God only knew how many more stretched before us. Tempers were beginning to make themselves evident. I thought this a wise precaution on Johnson's part, what you'd call perhaps a stitch in time.

A couple of the crew put up the small tent we'd fetched along for Merrilee. No quips were passed and few words spoken as a couple of the other hands prepared to ride circle.

Cow chips were unsuccessfully hunted to build up cook's fire, and he was forced in the end to accept an offering of greasewood stems.

When Plaza had the meal ready we swilled it down without talk. And those not otherwise employed sought their blankets. It was cooler up here with a gritty wind blowing up off the night-hidden desert, and I couldn't help wondering what would be the end of this harebrained exploit.

I had had it ground into me a long time ago that violence breeds violence, and Stovepipe's pithy observations relative to deserters looked like opening a new can of worms, as though we didn't have enough to nag at us already.

So far, however, we had seen no sign of pursuit—but it wasn't likely that we would with a day or two still left before Sneed fetched the sheriff out there. That feller was going to be madder than hops when he came out to gobble up Merrilee's horses and didn't find even a foal left behind.

We'd lost three foals yesterday in all that heat, and another the day before.

You'd have thought they were Merrilee's bosom beaus! She didn't say anything but her face told the story. She was plenty torn up about it. Everybody knew it.

"A trek of this kind you got to expect some losses," Johnson told her gruffly. "Just be glad they wasn't grown horses."

I could see this wasn't a heap of consolation. Another day dragged past.

In the cool of the evening—after dark, actually—we set off again, her and Johnson up in the lead, and setting, I thought, a more rugged pace though maybe, after that layoff, I only just imagined it. We still had them at a walk but it seemed more stretched out, and they weren't as closely bunched.

We covered a good twenty miles that night.

And when the sun came up, right after we'd finished eating, Durphy spied a rider approaching, and Johnson swore. "Here's a find kettle of fish!" he growled. I had no trouble catching his thought.

"You think he'll carry tales?" Durphy muttered, and Johnson slanched him a withering look.

"Howdy," the fellow said, riding up and casting an admiring eye over Merrilee's horses. "Looks like you folks are movin'."

Johnson shifted a mite. His shoulder moved, and flame wreathed the muzzle of the gun in his hand.

Chapter Four

Incredulity stared from Durphy's blanched cheeks. Merrilee, eyes enormous, stood rooted in shock as the stranger, doubling forward from knees unable any longer to support him, abruptly toppled and rolled half over.

"Too dead to skin," Joe Lucie noted and, as though those words broke the horrid spell, Merrilee flew at her foreman, furious.

"To kill that man in cold blood!" she cried. "To throw him away like a piece of waste paper! How could you *do* such a terrible thing?"

Johnson caught pounding fists in a rope-scarred hand.

"When you made up your mind to run off with them horses you put every neck in this outfit at risk. Horse stealin', my girl—"

"They were *mine*. Every one of them!"

"Some might take a different view. That bank, for instance. An' the law they've prob'ly put on our trail." Johnson's voice was calm as a millpond. "That bird would have talked, seein' a sight like this, an' before you could git out of bed tomorrer what he saw would be all over this country."

She stared, confused, tangled up in her thinking.

"This ain't no sideshow for people to gawp at." He let go of her wrists and, turning away, said, "Couple of you rannies start diggin' me a hole."

Lucie and Red Durphy got a pick and a shovel out of the supplies and began their excavating where Johnson pointed. "Faint heart never won fair lady," Johnson yapped, and the pair set to with a little more muscle.

Next time I glanced round Merrilee had vanished, gone into the seclusion of her tent, I reckoned. Johnson said to me while the rest of the crew was off caring for those *caballos,* "That feller look like a rancher to you?"

"Cowpuncher more likely. Don't reckon he'll be missed straight away, anyhow."

"That's all right then. Once he's planted I'll run them bangtails over the spot."

"You must of felt pretty sure of me."

The foreman cracked his lips in that lazy grin. "Had you pegged right from the start, bucko," and dropped his glance to my cutaway holster before bringing it up in that slanch-ways probe again. "You're old enough to know a man does what he has to."

I couldn't find anything to say to that, being no more anxious to court rumors than he was. To let that galoot get away with what he'd seen could have busted up this deal before we'd hardly got started. Just the same I couldn't like it. I expect we countenance a lot in this life that takes a deal of swallowing. I'd better remind myself to remember this fellow Johnson was built on a hair-trigger and favored snap decisions.

Two or three times before we left that place every horse in the outfit was run over the new-made grave till you couldn't tell it from anywhere else. But at last the boss was satisfied. The fellow's mount had been driven off, saddle and all, to be found anyplace but where we had camped. Wasn't a thing any one of us could have done to prevent it once Johnson latched onto the necessity for killing him.

Slogging along in the drag next morning, out of the hills and back in black rocks again, I was not much surprised when Red Durphy rode up and fell in alongside. That something was chewing him was evident. Scowling and squirming around in his stirrups, after riding some minutes in this sultry manner he let go all holds and said straight out, "Wish to hell I'd never signed on with this crackpot outfit!"

Meant that, I reckoned, to be taken at face value.

But I had sized him up long since for the sort you don't want to set much store by. The kind that delights in stirring up trouble and, wherever he can, slipping a chunk under it.

"A bit late for regrets, ain't it?"

His look jumped to me in an affronted stare. "That numbskull girl is like to get us all killed!"

"Some of us might get clear," I grinned.

Durphy swore. "If you can figure how, I'll be right behind you."

Yes, I thought, that's where you'll be all right. Safely tucked behind somebody else. Aloud I said, "Have to see what turns up, won't we?" and watched him ride muttering off up the line.

He was not a sort I liked to be around.

But like the rest I was stuck with him, and the rest weren't much better to my way of thinking. Merrilee Manton had surrounded herself—or been surrounded—with a prize crew of beauties. The caliber of men you might, sometime earlier, have looked to find riding with Quantrell.

A depressing thought.

Well, consider . . . Joe Lucie, scarred only with the past he kept to himself but an obvious scoundrel. Gil Plaza, our Spanish cook, who looked like a broken-down bullfighter.

Skinny Skeeter Jones, still more kid than man and with the punk talk of one dragged up in the streets. Angel Contrado with the face of a saint and the edgy hand of a none-too-sure gunslinger. Dirk Horba with a knife in his boot and another inside the back of his collar. Plus loud Red Durphy, perhaps most dangerous of the lot. I ticked them off in my head with a grimace.

And over them, as foreman, burly Stovepipe Johnson, who could probably bend bar iron between those rope-scarred fists and would do what he "had to do" according to his notions.

I said "Well" again. No one had forced me to join this outfit.

Back in Texas I'd been in and out of a whole flock of things. One thing I'd never been was a horse thief, and in this country nothing was counted lower.

Which switched my mind back on Durphy. Regardless of any bait he threw out he wasn't fixing to leave us. He meant to stay with these horses until they were disposed of. I'd seen the way he looked at them, naked hunger in his strange yellow stare. There wasn't anything, I reckoned, that bugger wouldn't do to get his hands on them if he could do it without getting snuffed in the process.

I was still pushing him around through my head when Merrilee rode back and swung her mount in beside mine. "You're looking mighty pert, ma'am."

And she was. In those blue jeans and yellow blouse she made a picture worth framing. "Thanks," she said, "but I'm not feeling very nice. I can't get over Stovepipe hauling off and shooting that fellow—Oh, I understand his thinking . . . but *killing*—I don't think I'll ever get over seeing that poor fellow collapse like he did. Full of life one moment and the next—it's too horrible!" she cried, putting up both hands and covering her face.

I had the wit to keep my mouth shut, but barely.

After a time I put a clean handkerchief into her hand, and she dried her eyes. And after another half-mile or so managed to look at me, rather hesitantly, as if she wondered what I thought of her. I could see well enough it hadn't crossed her mind what she might be letting the rest of us in for.

Next time I slid a glance in her direction she'd recovered enough to straighten her face out. "These horses," I said casual as possible, "do you honestly think they're as good as they look?"

"They're top horses. They'll go like the wind."

"I've seen a few that will go like the wind. How will they do with the wind in their faces?"

"Some of them have been raced . . . the ones my father brought up out of Texas. We might not have a Judge Welch, a Texas Chief, or a Possum but there are horses in this bunch that can give a mighty good account of themselves."

I certainly hoped she was right. From where I sat we might have to find out. "And you're staking everything on finding a market at Goldfield?"

"Yes," she nodded. "I wouldn't care to sell all of them, but I would sell—be willing to sell—enough of them to get myself established there."

"You mean buy another place? You intend to go on breeding horses?"

"Of course." She looked at me rather oddly, I thought. "What else would I do with my life? Horses are all I know anything about."

"You could marry," I said, not looking at her. "In fact you could marry and still go on with your horse breeding."

"I'm in no position to become acquainted with the sort of man I would care to spend the rest of my life with."

"Well," I said without much confidence, "you're acquainted with me."

It took a little urging but I looked at her then and saw the astonishment reflected in her face. There may have been something else besides. I didn't have the gall to look that close.

"Not *that* well acquainted," she said and faced front again.

"I expect we will be," I said, "before we're done with this."

During the next seven days, three new foals were dropped to come gallivanting along beside proud mares. By this time we were well into Nevada, still a far piece from Searchlight but zeroing in on it as rapidly as might be. That was where—according to Durphy—we'd swing more to the west in our approach to gaudy, gusty Goldfield. And those wealthy nabobs Merrilee hoped would exchange gold for fast horses.

I had no idea if there was a track up there but I was amply aware of other uses fast horses could be put to, and frequently were. As a business venture it seemed reasonable to suppose she was on the right course. If we could manage to get there intact with these bangtails.

A big "if" to my thinking.

Since the killing Merrilee's foreman had made a few procedural changes. Merrilee no longer rode at the front of the column with Johnson. These last few days she was one of the flankers. I was still riding drag. Johnson, on one of the two stallions, rode half a mile ahead of the lead horses with Joe Lucie something like a mile ahead of him. This arrangement was intended to insure us against having any more strangers getting within gunshot. As an additional precaution he had one of the crew riding half a mile out at either side of the column; the other men of our outfit and Merrilee rode at either side of the loose horses to keep them in the formation he wanted.

Traveling now across reasonably level desert some four miles west of the river, these outriders were in more or less constant view. It was apparent to me Johnson intended taking no chances on having our force impaired by desertions. He rode with a Sharps rifle across his pommel. Nobody doubted his willingness to use it.

I reckoned all told, from the time we'd quit Rafter, it would take at least a month before—if ever—we sighted Goldfield. The whole idea behind the course Johnson laid was to keep away from roads, towns, and people. With but that one grisly exception we had thus far managed to do this.

Twice during the past week we'd sighted Indians. On both occasions Johnson had waved them away. I wondered what he would do if they appeared in force. I don't guess any of us could claim to be comfortable with that kind of thought breathing down our necks.

Up till now, anyway, we'd seen no sign of pursuit, nor was this a thing I had really expected. That pursuit was behind us I hadn't the least doubt, but with all the dodges Johnson had gone to lose them, hampered by having to unravel these tricks with the winds floating sand over our tracks as it was doing now, it seemed reasonable to suppose they might never encounter us. In any event it was something to hope for.

I didn't reckon Johnson was losing much sleep over that particular prospect.

Whatever else he might be I was convinced in my own mind that Merrilee's foreman was no damned fool. He was a man who looked ahead, and it was belief in this notion that caused about half of my disquieting moments. Who could say what the fellow intended? For all I knew when the time was ripe he might well be figuring on taking these horses away from us.

This was something to be kept in mind. With this kind of crew I couldn't see how Merrilee and I would be able to prevent it. He could leave us stranded anytime it suited him. Accidents in this kind of country were very easily arranged.

All I could do was to keep my eyes peeled, and in the last ditch try to make it as costly for him as I was able.

Chapter Five

Another three days dragged their weary lengths past.

Two additional foals had joined us now. When discovered in the morning, they were frisking around their mothers in great shape, viewing the world with all the challenge of the young.

On the next afternoon Red Durphy dropped back in his half-furtive manner to inform me at the tail of the procession that we had now come halfway to our destination.

Asked how he could be sure of that he showed me his twisted bravo's grin. "I been here before, I remember the lay of this country," he said in his blustery cocksure style. "I been around, Peep. I been to Bannock an' Bullfrog—I've heard the owl hoot."

"What kind of owl?" I asked to get him talking, hoping something useful might come out of his bragging.

"Well . . . that's tellin'. You string along with a feller that knows, and you could wind up with your pockets full of chips."

I had a pretty good notion what sort of chips a man would collect stringing his bets with Durphy's kind. "You been to Goldfield?" I asked, and Durphy bobbed his head like he owned half the place.

"Was there," he said in a confidential tone, "when they put on that big fight. Matter of fact, I helped arrange it—me an' Tex. Them days I had a small interest in the Gold Dust Saloon. We had some high old times, I can tell you."

I managed to exhibit an admiring glance. "Expect you know a mort of people up there . . . mine owners, high rollers, prominent people in all walks of life. Expect you knew Death Valley Scotty?"

"Yeah. Knew him well. Used to stay with him sometimes when things got dull around town. Had a reg'lar castle out there in the roughs. Half the town was tryin' to find where his mine was. Once when I was out with him we seen a bunch campin' on our trail—never phased Scotty. He figured long's he had a four-mile lead he could lose the best of 'em. Had cans of water cached out all over."

"How long since you been up that way?"

"Well . . . let's see . . . must be three-four years, but I can see it now, can almost hear them ticker tapes clickin'. Best damn town in the West fer makin' money."

"They got a race track?"

"Don't know what they got now. They had a little bush track scraped outa the desert when I was there—horses runnin' every Sunday afternoon. Lot of matched races. One feller had a horse called Coal-Oil Johnny—come away from that track one evenin' with every pocket bulgin'," Durphy said. "Found him next mornin' stone cold dead out back of some saloon."

"What happened to the horse?"

"Killed him, too."

"You must have seen some wild times."

"You bet! That's where it was at. Anything you can think up, Goldfield had it."

"Must've been some pretty fancy jewelry floating around with all that mazuma."

"You never seen the like! Set in silver, set in gold, some of it even set in platinum! One of the Tucson silversmiths, Jimmie Herald, the Navajo—he's a ol' man now; he was there fer a while in his younger days 'fore he started workin' for Frank Patania. I've seen some of his stuff you couldn't buy today—worked mostly in turquoise, Jimmie did. One of the best—stuff he did for Patania sold all over Europe. Don't guess Jimmie ever made much out of it but ol' Frank made a bundle—everybody wanted it."

Durphy shook his head. "I better be gittin' on up the line."

Five days later we saw Indians again. Paiutes, Durphy called them.

There was nine in the bunch. They went round our horses three-four times at a pretty good clip, careful to keep outside Winchester range. "Lookin' 'em over," Durphy said. "Lookin' to see if we're fixed for trouble. Countin' us up. Good thing the boss ain't wearin' no dress."

"Reckon they'll try to cut out a few ponies?"

"Naw. Not now. Just sizin' 'em up. They like better odds. Terrain right here ain't favorable. More their style to set up a ambush," Durphy said in his man-of-the-world fashion. " 'Nother thing, Injuns as a rule ain't too fond of gettin' in their licks when the sun's shinin' down on 'em."

Johnson came larruping his horse from somewhere up beyond the front of the column, pulling up in a slather of dust. "Git up where you belong," he told Durphy, "an' get that rifle out from under your leg!"

He looked after Red, scowling, before turning to me. "Them fellers look hostile?" He looked off to where the Indians sat on their ponies eyeing Merrilee's horses.

"Red didn't think so. Says they're just givin' us the once-over."

"Cookin' up deviltry," Johnson growled. "You got any notion what tribe they're from?"

"They're Paiutes, accordin' to Red. I can't tell you one from the other. All I know firsthand about red men is you prod them, they'll prod back."

Johnson snorted. "When I prod somethin' that's the end of it. Injuns ain't no different from snakes," he declared, lifting that single-shot buffalo gun.

I reached out a fist. "All they've done so far is look at us. Unless you want a war on your hands, you'll put up that Sharps and get on with our legitimate business, which is gettin' these horses to Goldfield."

He gave me a hard and ugly look. Spinning his horse around on hind legs he went barreling on up the line in a temper that did not bode well for our future relations. In no time he had the whole column on the move again, sensibly holding it down to a walk. With a goosequill feeling along my spine, never twisting my head to find out what those buggers were up to, I swung in behind the last of our charges like there weren't any redskins within ten miles.

But this didn't mean I'd forgot about them.

One thing high up on any Indian's priorities is horses. And most especially white men's horses. I reckoned they'd be drooling over the memory of this bunch till they were finally driven into some sort of action. Not today certainly. Maybe not tomorrow. But sooner or later we'd be seeing those buggers again, I thought gloomily. I doubted the sharpest vigilance would deter them. Johnson, I reflected, might even have been right in his notion of first strike and to hell with the consequence.

I even began wondering if any of our outfit would ever see Goldfield.

We did not make any camp that evening, just pushed

straight on through the desert night, pausing no longer than it took to feed.

Lack of water was becoming a real problem.

How Red Durphy managed to slip away from the column even in the dark I never found out, but slip away he did, and Johnson became aware of it. I heard the growl of his voice farther up the line, saw the black bulk of him looming off to the side of me. "You seen Durphy?"

"Not since it got dark."

I could feel his ugly stare boring into me.

"Goin' to tell you somethin', mister," he began in a threatening tone, but whatever it was he must have had second thoughts, for with no further words he put his mount round me and went off into the night on the column's far side.

We went into camp about an hour before dawn. He put Horba and Lucie to riding herd. Angel Contrado and me were picked for lookouts. Gil Plaza put up Merrilee's tent and, soon as it grew light enough to pick up dried cowflops, Johnson told the Spaniard to get some grub cooked up.

The horses were restless. Johnson fetched out the nose bags and gave them some oats and had finally to give them the last of our water. Which was nowhere near the amount they needed. We breakfasted in shifts. It had by this time become evident to all that Durphy was missing. This was bound to occasion talk.

It was just after Merrilee's foreman had announced we'd be resting the horses here for three-four hours that Durphy rode into camp with an Indian. "This here's Hungry Bill, an old Shoshone frien' of mine from when I was up in this country before. Lived all his life round here. For a dollar a day he'll come along with us and keep us in water."

It appeared Johnson could abide one Indian if his presence meant water. The old man could speak a kind of pidgin English, and Hungry Bill was quickly put on the payroll with no thanks to Red.

"How far to first water?"

The Shoshone told Johnson, "Mebbeso half day."

Johnson with a studying stare said, "Lead off, and you, Peep, go with him, well out ahead of us. Where I had Skeeter."

Hungry Bill had mismatched eyes, one of them blue and the other brown. These he ran over me with his brows up. When I motioned him on he turned his scrawny piebald horse and set off, pointing a mite more into the west than the course we'd been following.

In the shank of the afternoon he took me into a growth of hackberries, hardly a smudge in the miles of sand spread tanly ahead of us, and there, sure enough, was a spring-fed creek that went back underground within a hundred yards. Cool, clear rippling water. No white man would have come within a mile of the place. I got down for a drink and let my horse have a little one. Hungry Bill showed the snags of his teeth in a wolfish grin. "Pretty good, huh?"

"Pretty good," I said, and rode out of this half-pint oasis to signal the rest of our outfit in.

Chapter Six

Since there were nothing but animal tracks in the vicinity, no evidence of recent use by the two-legged variety, Johnson, after a good look around, deemed it expedient to spend the night there. The supplies were unloaded, all the waterbags were filled and would have been hung on the tree limbs to cool in the breeze had I not pointed out the folly of advertising.

"Jesus Christ!" Johnson growled, and the bags came down.

Skeeter Jones put up Merrilee's tent in what little shade was available, then set out to hunt chips for Gil Plaza's supper fire while the Spaniard dug out his pots and pans.

As the evening drew on and three by three the horses took their turn to drop muzzles in the creek, Durphy, with his head back, appeared to be studying the hazed-over sky. "Might catch a rain," he informed the less educated.

"No rain," said the Indian from long experience. "Rain next month here."

For chow Plaza gave us corned beef from cans and refried beans from other cans, biscuits as fluffy as a bagful of feathers and java to wash it all down with.

I'd have liked mighty well to have been on better terms with Merrilee, but seemed like I'd two strikes against me right off the bat, having seen her so to speak with her hair down and being myself a hombre, the half of whom was Mex. I wouldn't say she looked down on that side of me, understand, but after all when you're out of the top drawer . . .

Understanding—even sometimes sympathizing with—divergent views had ever been the curse of my life. It certainly got me no place to be able to see myself from where she stood and consider me less than satisfactory, as I was sure she did. Very heartily did I despise the gringo assumption of superiority, and too much of the time discovered myself secretly deferring to it. Trying to get things straight in my head I once asked Gil Plaza about his reactions to *Norteamericanos*. Settling a comforting hand on my shoulder, the old fellow said with kind of a chuckle, "I laugh at their hypocrisies."

I suspect I wasn't yet grown enough to share so dispassionate a stance.

It must have been well after midnight and myself no closer to sleep than I'd been when I came off watch two hours ago when of a sudden I was jerked to attention by what seemed the sound of a turning pebble. It snapped my head around and brought me onto an elbow half off the ground to stare through the murk at Merrilee's tent where it backed against the deeper black of the trees. The trees were between myself and the tent, and I thought to catch some shift in the shadows.

Hauling off my boots I was afoot in an instant, gun in hand, moving warily nearer till I was close enough to make out the bent-over shape hovering there at the back of her tent.

At first, for a moment, I imagined it was Horba, but despite the glint of the knife he was holding, the shape was too skinny for Horba. It had to be Skeeter Jones, I realized, and, just as he was about to start his knife down the canvas, I belted him back of an ear with my gun barrel, hard enough in my fury to put this guttersnipe in a very bad way.

Not a sound came out of him, but that outstretched arm as the fellow collapsed slithered over the canvas and drew a gasp of alarm from inside the tent. Not being anxious at this time of night to provoke a storm of questions, I got myself away from the vicinity as rapidly as might be.

As the outfit was next morning fixing to tackle Plaza's grubpile, Johnson, having a good look at us, broke the sad tidings. "May as well tell you we're a man short this morning. Sometime during the night Skeeter Jones took the notion of carving a slit in the side of that tent. Somebody else bashed his head in. Since none of our number"—and he looked around again—"would want to be a party to polluting the neighborhood, a couple of you better get him buried, and pronto. We'll be pulling out of here in just about forty minutes."

There were plenty of sidelong looks passed about but I expect no one truly wanted to know who had done for poor Skeeter. It was an object lesson of undeniable threat to anyone inclined to put their nose inside that tent. For the moment at least I reckoned Merrilee was safe. And there'd be one less scoundrel making the rounds of our camps at night.

Thirty-five minutes after Johnson's announcement our outfit was on the move, Hungry Bill at the head of the column well out in front, Johnson next, and after him the loose horses and pack animals toting our supplies—now at about half strength—flankers at both sides of the column with me, as usual, eating dust at the rear.

Another hot day.

As we toiled along across the tawny sand beneath a brassy sky through those windless hours, I wasted no thought on the life I had snuffed. We chewed jerky for lunch without getting out of our saddles. It must have been about the middle of the afternoon when Johnson sent Merrilee up to the front and himself dropped back to ride a while beside me.

"Pretty dusty back here," he offered. "Guess you'd be happier along one of the flanks."

"I'm all right."

"Who do you reckon staved Skeeter's head in?"

He didn't look at me when he asked this. I didn't look at him either. "Hard tellin'," I said. "But that canvas had a cut in it—I noticed when I was packin' it up. I doubt if anyone tries to make it bigger."

Johnson nodded, sleeving sweat off his chin. "What do you suppose he was up to? Skeeter, I mean."

"Expect your guess is good as mine." I sleeved sweat off my own. "You got any idea how far off Goldfield is?"

"Hungry Bill says we've passed Searchlight. Nothin' ahead now till we hit Lathrop Wells. Which we'll damn sure skirt. Northwest from there some thirty miles is the town of Beatty. Accordin' to his figurin'—for whatever that's worth—Goldfield's roughly a hundred miles north. Say a couple hundred miles from where we're at now."

"Yeah. Roughly twenty days. If we don't shrivel up and blow away first."

Johnson said, "It ain't the miles that's gittin' under my skin. It's these buggers we're travelin' with and them god-dam Paiutes." He stared ahead for three-four minutes, then growled in disgust. "She couldn't pay enough to hire top hands. I done the best I could. All we've got is the scrapin's. Ain't a man in this outfit wouldn't take off with them horses if he thought he could git away with it! The trash we've got is what pirates is made of!"

"You're probably right about that. But lackin' a leader I doubt they've got the guts to jump you. They'd all have to be in it together, and I can't see that happening."

"What about Durphy?"

"I think we better keep an eye on him. He's ornery enough. Under certain conditions I believe he could be dangerous. But engineerin' a coup? I don't think he's got it in him."

Johnson's hard stare quartered my face. "You could do it."

"Not my style."

"I wish by God I could believe that!"

There was a bitterness in his look and tone that plainly told the strain he was under. The harsh planes of his cheeks showed the hardness that had been ground into him. That chin-strapped hat accented his toughness. The squashed nose, the forward throw of his bristly chin were visible tokens of the foreman's unswervable stubbornness. I couldn't doubt, so long as a shred of life remained in him, he'd go through with whatever he set his hand to. I was thankful to feel Merrilee had in him an abiding loyalty, a man who had her best interests at heart.

"Like you," I said, "I'll be doing my best to make sure she ain't left holdin' the short end of this stick."

"All right," he growled. "I don't know you from Adam but I'll take your word for it."

After he'd gone back to the front of the column some of the tension I'd felt in him stayed with me. A lot could happen in two hundred miles to a party no larger than ours traveling strange country with a fortune in horseflesh. We had set ourselves a near impossible task and up to now had been extraordinarily lucky.

Too much luck, I thought, to last.

Like Johnson I was edgily distrustful of the Rafter crew. I felt they were capable of just about anything but concerted action. What they might do if we were set upon by redskins was highly problematical. If the opportunity presented itself it was my dire hunch they would bolt with as many of the horses as they could manage to latch onto.

I believed this in keeping with their kind of people. And I could come up with no way to prevent this. In the world of rogues and scalawags it was dog eat dog and every man for himself. Examining the situation we had got ourselves into I was forced to conclude it was like to boil down to being us three—Merrilee, Johnson, and myself—against the world. And the way it looked now it seemed powerful easy for us to become buzzard bait.

We knew nothing about that Shoshone we'd hired to lead us to water. Any friend of Durphy's was highly suspect. Hungry Bill's presence could easily be some facet of a plot Durphy had rigged to part us from these horses. We knew nothing of the relations between Shoshones and Paiutes—Indians were forever squabbling among themselves, but when the stakes appeared sufficiently advantageous they could act in concert as they had at the Little Bighorn. Front and center in my thinking was the redskins' love of horseflesh. Considering our situation in such a context it was not at all difficult to see Hungry Bill leading us into a prearranged trap.

These were some of the more pregnant thoughts that cluttered my head during the following week. I might have all the trappings of an unlettered cowhand but when my old man, Toribio Teclo Boyano, was in the chips my mother, whom he loved dearly, had insisted I get a good education. A great deal of this in the years of my wanderings had gone into the discard in favor of protective coloring. I'd done a lot of foolish things in that time but had learned that regrets seldom buttered any parsnips, and with Khayyám had come to feel one thing was certain, the rest but lies.

As we drew ever nearer Lathrop Wells, Johnson's look, it seemed to me, grew daily grimmer, more saturnine and testy. I became convinced this was not the first time he'd been here. Hungry Bill might, and often did, fetch us to water but it was Stovepipe Johnson who each day set our course anew, picking our route by remembered things out of his past.

Filled with disquieting notions, one night after grub I got him aside with a demand to be told what canker was eating him, and I could see he was minded to put me off.

"If you're banking on me for help in this deal and you know more than I do," I said to him bluntly, "I ought to be told what's botherin' you."

He rubbed a hand over his jowls, staring off into the dark as though listening to things I could not hear. "The hell of it is I don't know," he growled finally.

"You've been lookin' all week like death warmed over. You act like a man with some kind of ugly hunch you can't shake."

"That's about the size of it," he nodded. "Nothin' you can put your finger on. Last time I was round these parts there was a hell's smear of Injuns camped out at the Wells. I was goddam lucky to get clear with my hair."

"Don't seem likely they'd be there now."

"That's what I been tellin' myself."

I nodded. "Problem is you don't believe it. Can't we go around them Wells?"

"Best way round is to swing well south. But south's strange country I never been into. I don't know if there's a way through or not," he said worriedly.

"We'll just have to try it and see, I reckon. Wait here. I'll fetch Hungry Bill. Maybe he can tell us."

The Shoshone was dozing alongside the fire with an old blanket draped over his scrawny shoulders. "Bill," I said, "the boss wants to powwow," and he followed me back to where I'd left Johnson.

Merrilee's foreman said, "Bill, what's south of Lathrop Wells?"

"Heap bad country."

"Bad how?"

"All on end. Lotta rock. Gullies and canyons—bad place."

"Can we get through?"

The Indian shrugged. "Mebbeso." He didn't look enthusiastic. "Many cliffs."

"What about water?"

"One place." Bill showed bad teeth in what passed for a grin.

"Going north through here—how many miles?"

"Maybe ten."

"How about Injuns?"

"No Injuns there."

Red Durphy came out of the dark to join us. "Why don't we go through the Wells like everyone else?"

"We don't care to go through the Wells," I told him.

"Why not?"

"That's why not," Johnson said with his face tight.

"Like to take us a couple days to get through them badlands. That country's cut up all to hell an' gone. Outside the Devil's Playground that's as bad a stretch as you're like to find. And hot—my Gawd, it's worse'n Death Valley."

I looked at Johnson. He said in a tone that brooked no argument, "That's where we're goin'."

Durphy, glancing at the Indian, shrugged. "Well, don't say you wasn't warned." He hitched up his pants and walked off where he'd come from. Johnson told Hungry Bill, "Set a course for that place when we leave here in the morning."

Chapter Seven

Two days' travel on this new heading took us into no badlands. This inclined me to hope the devious Durphy and his Shoshone friend had been feeding us more lies in their intention of taking us past Lathrop Wells. A third day's travel found us still moving across this rolling stretch of tawny sand without even so much as a bush in sight. Johnson's anxiety began to abate until on the fourth day he seemed almost his old unflappable self.

Along toward the middle of that fourth afternoon we began to encounter wind-riven ridges grown up about rabbit brush and scrubby manzanita. Outcrops of rock appeared here and there among patches of sage. Two hours before dark Hungry Bill loped back from his advanced position to declare we had better make camp and close-herd the bangtails.

Johnson, with his face toughening up, rode off with him to have a look. Returning presently to where we waited with the horses, Johnson declared, "We'll camp here till morning. Unload the supplies."

Off to one side I saw Durphy and Angel Contrado with their heads together.

While Joe Lucie was putting up Merrilee's tent, her foreman gave me a beckoning look, and Durphy followed me over to hear what he had to say. Johnson beat around no bushes. "Up ahead," he said, "the ground drops away into a great hole. We can get down there but it's going to be tricky with all these loose horses—"

"I warned you," Durphy grinned. "Don't say I didn't tell you how it would be!"

"I've heard," Johnson said, "about enough out of you." In that craggy face his stare shone black as ebony. "If you've been down there you can lead the way with that Shoshone when we start off tomorrow. And I'm tellin' you right here an' now at the first sign of double-dealin' you better prepare to meet your Maker."

When we set off next morning Johnson made a few changes. I was told to join Merrilee and Contrado on the right flank of the column. Horba, who'd been accustomed to riding that flank, was moved to the opposite side with Joe Lucie and Gil Plaza, Johnson taking over my spot at the rear.

It was slow and hot work getting those horses down the face of that drop and hotter still when finally we got to the bottom and sat staring at the awful landscape ahead of us. Red rocks reared up in every direction, some of them forty to fifty feet high, and the view got no better as we squirmed our way forward, strung out like a train of ants through an unholy tangle of sun-blasted gullies and cliff-sided canyons.

High overhead in a brassy sky the black shapes of buzzards sailed in vigilant circles. Half a dozen times in the course of that morning we got into box canyons whose only way out was the way we'd come in. We rode that day in what amounted to a crawl, forced by the terrain to be constantly alert in that debilitating heat lest a horse be crowded into the jut of some rock and, as could so easily happen, snap a leg.

Hungry Bill's prognostication of taking two days to get through this grotesque maze of fantastic red rock began to seem a gross understatement. Twice during that terrible day we stopped to water the horses from our hats. No faintest breeze stirred the furnacelike heat, and I worried that Merrilee might collapse, but she was stronger than she looked. Any number of preposterous notions crept into my head during the nightmare hours we toiled through that labyrinth, chief among them the conviction that Johnson for some unguessable reason had deliberately put us into this ghastly predicament.

It must have been close to five when the horses began to prick up their ears, some of them whinnying as they went hurrying forward, giving us fits trying to keep them from crowding each other against the rocks rearing up on both sides of the passage.

Abruptly we found ourselves in a kind of saucerlike bowl that was free of rocks, with grass underfoot and a shallow spring-fed stream rippling across its center. For about ten minutes we had our hands full keeping the loose horses from running over each other in their eagerness to get at the water. And harder still was the task of keeping them from foundering. But somehow we managed, though I'd sooner take a beating than go through that again.

We set up our camp, refilled the water bags, gamboled in that creek like a bunch of fool kids and, after a first-rate meal dished up by Plaza, with no fear of the horses straying, stretched out bone-weary for the soundest sleep we'd had since leaving Rafter.

Fortified by a good hearty breakfast of *frijoles y chili*, we were packed up and off to tackle the rest of this devilish route by seven o'clock with the morning already beginning to heat up. Hungry Bill and Red Durphy took the lead as before, guiding us through the twists and turns of that looping trail that in more than a few places closed us in like a chute with scarcely room for one horse to shuffle through at a time.

By noon a thermometer, if we'd had one with us, must have shown the temperature at one hundred and twenty if not more. The rocks seemed to swim in the shimmer of heat writhing off them. By two o'clock the way grew more open, and we began our climb toward the distant rim, which we reached and staggered over just short of dark.

Certainly all of us, I guess, were mightily relieved to get out of these bottoms. I know I was. There was a breeze up here, and the contrast in temperature, though still pretty warm, felt almost cool by comparison—I even pulled on my brush jacket before setting up Merrilee's tent. The horses once again were cautiously watered and not given any feed until they'd cooled out. I felt as though I'd been yanked through a knothole and reckoned the rest must have felt about the same.

Contrado and Durphy went wandering off in a search for fuel for Plaza's supper fire, and Johnson went to have a confab with Merrilee to which I wasn't invited. So I helped Plaza dig out his supper things and afterward, since the pair hunting cow chips had not yet returned, I broke off an armful of creosote canes to get him started.

The sun went down in a blaze of glory, coloring a reef of clouds along the western horizon. Shadows stretched long and dark across an arid terrain that was thinly freckled with bunchgrass clumps so dry and brittle they would break at a touch.

The missing pair came back with empty hands, Durphy appearing smug as a cat filled with quail. I made out not to notice and broke off another batch of stems for the Spaniard's fire.

After the horses had been fed and we'd filled our bellies, Merrilee, coming up to me, suggested walking around for a bit, which we did, and it came into my mind once again how she'd looked when I'd first seen her back at Rafter.

Out of earshot of the others she said, sounding thoughtful, "Perhaps I was wrong deciding to take my horses to Goldfield. Johnson tells me we lost two more foals and a mare coming through that awful hole. It makes me sick just thinking about it."

"Well, you did what you figured you had to do, I expect. In your place I might have done the same. Pretty hard thing to see the work of years pass into the hands of a man like Phil Sneed. I know you love every one of them."

"Yes, I do—it's why I take it so hard when we lose one. That mare was one of our very best. Old Sheba. Fourteen she was . . . like one of the family." She paused and a nostalgic look came over her face and, among other things I guessed, she was likely remembering and thinking about her father and about how he'd been killed and how he'd been missed, and the responsibilities dumped on her shoulders for keeping the ranch going with no one to lean on but old iron-jawed Johnson. "I practically grew up with Sheba," she said. "I guess it's silly to feel as I do over the loss of an animal."

"Don't seem silly to me," I told her. And the loss of a father, close as they'd evidently been, must have been a real wrench. I knew nothing, of course, about her mother and had no memory of her having been mentioned. "Sometimes," I said, "an animal can assume more importance than most of the persons one rubs shoulders with. I cried for days when somebody stepped on a baby turtle I had. Goes to show what a kind heart you have."

She looked at me gratefully, and I raked my mind to come up with something that might gain me some additional ground with her. But I found those brown eyes just then exceedingly hard to meet and broke off my search in some confusion as she asked with a glint of amusement, "Which side of your nature dredged up that solace?"

"Mex'kin side," I ruefully muttered. "More *simpático—*

haven't you noticed? Put a Mex and a gringo side by side, it's the Mex that'll jump to help every time. *Norteamericanos* take after them folks in Christ's time that crossed to the other side of the road."

"Well! Are you calling me a Philistine?"

Looked like I'd put my foot straight into it, and I was some tangled up in myself til I saw the laughter bubbling up in her glance and discovered I'd been had and this was nothing but teasing. "Seriously," she said, "why do you suppose Johnson insisted on taking us through that terrible hole? Look at the horses—they're all gaunted up."

"Expect that trip had a lot to do with it but the lack of green fodder and not enough oats is part of the problem. He remembered the Wells as the camping ground for Indians, and you know how redskins are about horses. Rather have horses than gold any day. He took us through those rocks because he was told there wasn't no other way around. Don't sell him short. He's rough an' gruff an' says what he thinks but it's in my mind he's plumb devoted to your best interests."

She didn't appear to be more than half convinced, and I was searching my head for a more telling argument when she said, with brown eyes probing my face in that direct unnerving way she had, "How would you like to have his job?"

"Me?" That pretty near threw me. "You oughtn't to swap horses in the middle of the stream. Don't cross him up. I doubt we could manage to pull through without him."

She waved that aside. Said impulsively, "I'd trust *you*, Peep." She put a hand on my arm in a way that made my insides churn. "I think I'd trust you—"

"Well you shouldn't," I grumbled, trying to be honest. "You don't know me from Adam. For all you know . . . well, hell . . . I doubt I could measure up. My heart an' head don't always ride the same trail. I'd try mighty hard but I'm a mixed-up notional sort of a jigger. You stick with Johnson. He's got a one-track mind."

Chapter Eight

Maybe I didn't try hard enough; I seldom went beyond my own best interests. Still I hated to see that old bastard sold short by the very person he was risking his life for. I couldn't see him doing this for gain and did my best to make her see this, though I reckoned she had likely been brought up to consider her old man's hired help as no better than servants to be ordered around but not taken seriously. I doubt it had ever occurred to her they had hopes and aspirations of their own. I suspected she still resented that handful of home truths he had thrown at her just before we'd left Rafter.

I could feel her stare digging into my face. Now she said hesitantly, "That night outside my tent . . . was it you killed Skeeter?"

"Water under the bridge," I grunted. "You stay with Stovepipe or we'll never see Goldfield. I'm backin' his hand all the way. This ain't his first trip into this country. He'll have contacts up there—folks he's acquainted with; probably knows the people you'll want to do business with. When it comes to Nevada I'm just a green hand."

Her grip on my arm seemed to get a mite tighter. "But he's not in love with me."

I licked dry lips. "Not so sure about that. I think he looks on you as the daughter he never had. Don't forget it was him came out of Texas with your father. Helped him collect the start of these bangtails you set such store by. If your father trusted him you ought to be willin' to."

With her body turned fencepost still in the shadows she said, "Let's go back. It's getting cold out here."

Came over me later that was some kind of hint. She let go of my arm to retrace our steps, and the moment was lost. It was darker now, and as we headed for the fire I felt the need to say something but couldn't figure what nor find any words that might have made sense. I felt like a chump—like I'd been handed an opportunity I'd sadly mismanaged.

She didn't stop by the fire but went on to her tent without a backward look. I was still staring after her when Red Durphy came sidling up to say, "Better luck next time," and seeing that grin I damn near hit him.

We broke camp before daylight and by midmorning had covered close to six miles with the column strung out and Johnson with Hungry Bill at the head of it and myself once again bringing up the rear. Merrilee I reckoned was out on one of the flanks, same as Durphy, Horba, Lucie, and Plaza. The cook's job at times like these was to keep an eye on the packs. Our supplies had been considerably diminished and to lose even one at this stage could damn well be a disaster.

I wondered where Angel Contrado had got to. Couldn't recall seeing him since this morning, and that brought back last evening's view of him and Red Durphy wandering off to hunt stuff for Plaza to build up a fire with and coming back later without any. What had that pair been up to? Some sort of mischief, I told myself scowling.

Contrado, with that unworldly face of a saint, was, to my mind, a thoroughgoing rascal. In a situation like this he might well be as dangerous to the rest of us as Durphy. For them to team up in anything could be bad news.

But, mostly, the thoughts I had that grabbed for attention had to do with Merrilee and myself in relation to her. I wasn't exactly down and out, though compared to her place in the social scale and the wealth represented by this batch of top horses, I was strictly a nobody and with my mexed parentage probably hadn't a chance of being more to her than I was right now.

It was a miserable notion I couldn't come to terms with.

Even a beggar could peer at a queen if he wasn't caught doing it. But this and other fantasies that crept through my thinking did very little to improve my outlook. She knew all right how I felt about her but I couldn't isolate one single occasion I could honestly feel had been intended to encourage me. I was one of the hired hands and saw damn little hope of ever being more.

Lucie rode back to see how I was making out, appearing abruptly out of the dust. "How's it goin'?"

"Good enough, I guess. You seen Angel?"

"Now you mention it, don't guess I have. Ain't he with us?"

"Can't seem to remember havin' seen him this morning."

"Reckon he just up an' quit?"

"Keep your eyes peeled," I said. "Him and Durphy was pretty chummy yesterday."

"They've been chummy before."

"Durphy's got his eye on those bangtails. He'd like mighty well to get away with a few."

"Come to that," Joe Lucie grinned, "I guess we all would."

"All of us ain't crooked enough to try it."

" 'Course not. Be pretty risky, wouldn't it, with Stovepipe packin' that buffalo gun? I'd sure hate to have it pointed my way."

"Yeah. If that pair are cookin' up something I'd advise you to stay out of it."

"You kin bet I will." He peered down at his boot tops. "Wouldn't want to wind up like Skeeter done."

We made a dry camp out in the mesquites that night and were on our way again just before daylight while the desert air was still cool enough to touch. Yesterday by my calculations we'd made better than twelve miles, which under the conditions seemed to me extra good. This morning I'd seen Durphy filling his face at Plaza's fire, acting just like he'd been with us all along.

He had authorized himself a new position along the left flank not more than a couple of rope lengths ahead of me. Deciding a few words might clear the air a bit I loped up there. He gave me a slanchways look. I said, "What have you and that angel-faced gunslinger been cookin' up?"

"I don't know what you're talkin' about."

"Where were you yesterday?"

He put on his mean look. "I been around."

I said, "Let me give you a small piece of advice—"

"You're not my keeper," he growled, looking ugly.

"Quite true. But if I find you mixed up in any attempt to cut out a few of Miz Manton's horses it will be the sorriest thing you ever tried in your life." I looked at him grimly. "And you can pass that on to Contrado next time you two get to chinnin' together."

When we camped that night near a spring the Shoshone had found for us, Johnson mentioned while we were eating that, to the best of his calculations, we were now within a hundred and fifty miles of our destination.

Horba wanted to know if we'd be passing through Tono-pah.

Johnson shook his head. "Not if I can find any way of avoiding it. What's on your mind?"

"There's mines around there. We could probably sell some of them nags without havin' to push 'em all the way to Goldfield."

"I reckon it's possible," Johnson nodded.

"Why don't we do it then?" Durphy piped up.

"Because we set out to take these horses to Goldfield and that's where they're goin'."

Contrado said then, "Could be we'll never get there."

"We'll get there," I said. "Might have to wade through a little gore. Might lose a few rannies along the way, but we'll get there."

"Could be some of that gore will come outa you." Contrado threw back with a fist on his gun handle.

Johnson was shaking his head at me but I was in no mood to take more of this horseshit. With Red Durphy about ten steps in front of me, Horba about double that off at my right, and Contrado, feet planted, about six feet to my left, I guess they figured I hadn't a Chinaman's chance against the three of them. I couldn't see Joe Lucie but this had gone too far for me to back down now. This was where they reckoned to eliminate me.

"You're all set. What're you waitin' on—a formal invitation?"

Chapter Nine

Horba in that moment appeared to grow short of breath. Caught trying to balance between temper and caution, a sudden apprehension widened the startled mismatched eyes. The grin fell off Contrado's mouth, and Durphy, tipped forward above a spread-fingered hand, took a half-step back with all the air leaking out of him. "Hell's fire," he gasped, "Can't you take a joke?"

"Is that what it was?"

"What else?" Horba said, trying hard to catch hold of that gone-away smile. And Contrado with the face of an agonized saint dredged up a laugh that couldn't have fooled anyone. "Of course," he grumbled. "You can't believe we were serious?"

"I think," Johnson growled, "it's time we called it a day. We'll be pullin' out tomorrow at five o'clock sharp."

Lucie said from behind me, cool as two frog legs in the same hand, "Who'll ride nighthawk for this outfit?"

"You for one," Johnson said, looking us over, "and Peep if he's able to keep his eyes open."

Dirk Horba, it was plain, wasn't satisfied yet. But though he put a contemptuous stare on the plot's ringleader he was obviously not planning to spark fireworks on his own. Stovepipe shooed them off toward their bedrolls, and I picked up my saddle and followed Lucie toward the loose-held remuda. "Guess I owe you somethin' for what happened back there."

"Not me," he denied. "I never so much as wiggled a finger."

I knew better, of course. If he'd had a gun on me I'd be damn well sorting through the heavenly harps and halos by this time. Be they ever so unwanted a man has to face up to his obligations, and I was convinced those guns had stayed sheathed out of more than any sudden fear of Peep Boyano.

After a breakfast of refried beans in the deepest black that precedes the half-light heralding dawn, Johnson allotted new positions for all of us. He had Merrilee up ahead with Hungry Bill, Lucie leading the column of bangtails, pack horses, and the rest of the remuda, with Plaza, Horba, and myself riding left flank and Contrado and Durphy on the other. There was no one bringing up the tail-end this morning. I reckoned it rather fortunate Merrilee wasn't aware of this. She had set off at once with our Shoshone guide, far enough ahead to be out of the way of flying lead in the event the aborted hostilities of last evening flared afresh.

Which was fine and dandy, far as it went, but left me uneasily pondering what might happen if a mile ahead of us they ran into redskins. As it turned out they, didn't, and at noon Johnson, ever alert to Merrilee's best interests, reshuffled the crew again.

For the rest of the day Horba and Plaza rode the right flank. Contrado and Lucie flanked the column's other side with Merrilee directly ahead of it, Hungry Bill riding solo well in advance. Red Durphy and I ate dust at the rear.

The clouds hung low beneath an overcast sky. No breeze enlivened the sultry air, muggy as dog days along the Ohio, yet certainly more comfortable than that intolerable heat we'd crawled through crossing those red rock bottoms. We glimpsed few cows, saw no horsemen at all, and went into camp with tempers untarnished.

It has often occurred to me what a blessing it is we're unable to look into the tomorrows ahead of us. By the simple grace of this dispensation we are saved considerable futile anguish. We rode through the next pair of days without incident.

On the third, having finished breakfast, we were starting to pack what was left of our supplies, Durphy ensconced in a fit of the sullens, when Horba began staring with an expressionless face out over our back trail and, beyond him, Merrilee, horrified, rigidly peering in the same direction.

A premonitory chill passed icy fingers along my spine as I whirled to behold a line of motionless horsemen drawn up and eyeing us scarcely a mile away. Johnson swore from a gone-dry throat. Contrado growled, "Those goddam Paiutes!"

There were about a dozen. Might easily be the ones who'd looked us over before.

"Do we give them the horses?" Lucie asked, likely just to be saying something.

Gil Plaza said, "I can see the glint of two-three guns. Do you think they'll come at us?"

"Not yet," Johnson said. "Ain't got enough edge way things stand right now. Get those pack horses loaded and we'll be on our way. We get into a fight here they'll scatter these horses to hell an' gone."

All day they followed, keeping their distance, dogging our tracks with a grim persistence. Just knowing they were back there keeping us in sight began to sharpen our tempers as the hours dragged past. Johnson held us to a walk. "Worst thing we could do is let 'em think we're scairt."

I doubt that any of us got much sleep that night.

When the sun climbed over the distant hills they were still

there back of us, watching and waiting. It was Merrilee who pointed out the next danger facing us. "Look!" she cried, and there northeast of us were a second ten or twelve.

I suggested skipping breakfast but Johnson shook his head. "It's their move," he grumbled. "We do everything same as usual. They know well as we do we can't fight them and keep hold of these horses."

Joe Lucie said, "That bunch to the north of us are starting to move. You see what they're doing? Gettin' between us and the way we been figurin' on going."

Hungry Bill was studying this new bunch. "All same—Paiutes. Get trail blocked."

And Johnson said: "Aimin' to drive us into the west unless we're prepared to fight, which we ain't." He asked the Shoshone, "What's west of here, Bill?"

"Daylight Pass," Red Durphy said, and the Shoshone nodded.

"Pass to what?"

"Death Valley," Red said.

"Damn!" Merrilee said. "We don't want to go there!"

"No choice," Contrado informed us, pointing southwest. There were eight more horsebackers spread out in that direction. All told there must have been thirty of those buggers waiting to shepherd us into Death Valley.

"Once we're into the pass," Durphy said, "we'll maybe be able to hold them off."

I didn't think it likely or they'd not be intending to drive us there, but I kept my mouth shut because we were no better fixed for a fight here than yesterday.

Plaza cooked up some grub, and we stood around eating and eventually packed up, and because, as Contrado had pointed out, our only choice was to go west or fight, we got under way. I had a strong and ever-increasing suspicion these Indians were after us at Durphy's invitation, some kind of a deal he and Contrado had hatched up. I even thought several times of confronting them with it, but any fight among ourselves would only hasten the inevitable. Too, I could be wrong; Durphy and Contrado might not have a thing to do with those Paiutes.

Johnson had reshuffled our positions once again. Only the Shoshone, Hungry Bill, was up front now. Merrilee and Joe Lucie rode the left flank, Plaza and Dirk on the right, but there was no way we could hold them off for long if they made a push to come at us. Merrilee, Johnson, and myself made hardly more than a token buffer.

"Why," asked Merrilee, looking more upset than I'd seen her, "do they want to chase us into Death Valley?"

I didn't know but Stovepipe said, "Not so apt to have their plans interfered with. That's a pretty desolate country. No cavalry patrols over there."

"But I thought all the Indians were on reservations."

"These buggers ain't."

He looked pretty grim.

They followed us all morning just out of rifle range and apparently content to keep their distance so long as we went in the desired direction. Twice our Shoshone tried to swing us back toward Goldfield, and both times the northernmost batch hastened to string out ahead. We could probably have broken through but not without a fight and the loss of too many horses.

"Thing is," Johnson said, "if we can't hold them off in the Pass and are forced down into Death Valley we may still have a chance of coming out of this if no guns are fired. There's a feller up at the north end I used to know pretty well—name's Scotty. Got a kind of stronghold up there if we can reach it."

By the middle of the afternoon the ground ahead began a long and scarcely discernible climb toward some fairly tall hills still blue in the distance. "That's where the Pass is at," Johnson muttered in an aside to me. "Near the top I think it gets pretty narrow."

"You reckon we'll get up there this side of night?"

"Afraid not, but in the dark our chances of defendin' it will be a heap better. Anyway, with them redskins on our tail we can't afford to stop till we're up there."

"I don't like it," Merrilee objected. "What you've got in mind is to send the horses through and then try to keep the Paiutes from following. You can't do it without shooting and soon as you start burning powder these horses—"

"They'll not scatter inside that gut," Johnson told her. "Shouldn't take more'n four of us to hold off them Injuns. Rest of us'll go with the horses."

I kept my mouth shut. What Stovepipe proposed was the only practical solution. A damn sticky mess any way you eyed it. We daren't send Durphy, Contrado, or Horba off with the *caballos* nor could we put any trust in them defending the Pass. If any one of them had hatched up a deal with these Paiutes, which it looked like, I reckoned we would end up losing the horses no matter what we did.

With this dismal prospect in mind I said, "Reckon I better have a talk with coosie," and before any protests could be aired I sent my horse loping on up the line.

The Spaniard, Gil Plaza, was old enough, I thought, to have had enough experience and enough common sense locked back of his reticent behavior to maybe be of real help in this predicament. He looked a little puzzled when I beckoned him away from Horba's hearing, but pulled off to the side waiting for me to come up with him. I was thankful Horba hadn't noticed.

"Gil," I said, "if you know anything about Horba, Red Durphy, or Contrado you think Johnson ought to savvy, I wish you'd tell him before them Indians decide to gang up on us."

"What could I know of them?"

"That's what I'm asking."

He shook his head and shrugged his indifference.

"Which one of them fetched those Paiutes down onto us?"

"I don't believe any one of them could do that."

"Those rascals have been hankering to get away with some of this horseflesh for as long as I've been with this outfit. Durphy disappeared for a while the other day. Contrado was gone for the most of one night. What were they up to? Haven't you any idea?"

"I can't imagine," Plaza said. "This is no time to stir up trouble in the outfit. If it's trouble you're hunting, those redskins will furnish about all we can handle."

Having said which, he crawled into a reticence I could not shake. Leaving me filled with frustration, he rode off to resume his position along the flank of the column.

I felt balked and angry and vaguely puzzled, too. I'd have given long odds he knew more than he'd acknowledged. When the others caught up with me Merrilee's foreman asked, "What did you find out? Is he on our side or ain't he?"

I gave him the gist of what the Spaniard had said, and Johnson snorted. "Not much help there."

Dark was not far off when we came into the ruggedest part of the climb with the hills spread around us in the gathering dusk. Johnson said, "If my memory's not haywire a couple more miles will take us right spang into the narrowest part." He looked round at Merrilee. "What's your intention? Do we shove the horses on through an' try to hold off them redskins?"

Biting her lip she turned to me. "What do you think, Peep?"

"You want it straight from the shoulder?"

"Of course," she said, eyes searching my face.

I stared at the cliffs piling up on both sides. "Four rifles up top might be able to hold them, but I doubt it. Way things stand now the only man in this crew who might go against the rest of 'em to join us is Joe Lucie, and I'd hate to gamble on him. If it was left to me I reckon I'd push on."

Looked like that had struck the right note with her. Staring back over my shoulder, I saw the three groups had now converged and were walking their ponies straight for the Pass, not hurrying a bit, satisfied, no doubt, that we could not escape them.

Probably we couldn't, but if they waited till morning to launch their attack there was a faint possibility we might elude them yet. Or at least find some place where their superiority of numbers would not immediately overwhelm us.

We eased Merrilee's horses through the gut at the top. By the time this was accomplished, full dark had arrived and there was no way of knowing what awaited us below or how far we'd have to travel to reach level ground. If there was any ahead of us. I put the question to Johnson.

"There's nothing ahead of us, near as I can recollect, that isn't about halfway to hell. Be damn hot and filled with mirages, dust, and desolation. Furnace Creek is down there someplace. Palm trees an' pools of water, but mostly it's just sand and gila monsters ringed by mountains, some of 'em more than eleven thousand foot high. And one stretch down there that's over two hundred and fifty foot below sea level that is hot enough to sear your eyeballs."

"Lovely prospect. Any place we can hide?"

Johnson shrugged. "Maybe. If we can find it ahead of the massacre."

It was plain he hadn't much hope of this. I said, "How big's this oven?"

He shrugged again. "Don't know if it's ever been measured. But I can tell you one thing. It'll be a tarnation long walk if we git shut of these horses."

"Can we take them through it?"

"God willin', but we'd be fools to count on it. Tonight we got to try an' shake off them Injuns."

"And you don't reckon we can?"

"I sure as hell don't. We might be lucky enough to lose 'em

for a while, but they can follow our tracks no matter where we go, and sooner or later they're goin' to come onto us."

"If we gave them the horses—?"

Merrilee cut in. "We're not giving these horses to anyone!"

"Wouldn't make no difference if we did," he said. "The white man figures the best Injuns is dead ones, and Injuns reckon dead palefaces ain't goin' to run off at the mouth. Hard lines, boy, but that's the way it is in this country."

There didn't seem to be much to say after that.

After about three hours we reached the bottom of the grade, and Johnson went larruping off to the front to tell Hungry Bill which way he expected him to take us. Unless Stovepipe stayed at the head of the column, I thought that Shoshone might find some direction that suited him better.

When Johnson came back he voiced the same notion. "I'm goin' to have to stay up at the front," he growled, "an' I think you better stay up there with me," he told Merrilee. "We'll leave Peep back here to catch any lead them buggers throw at us."

She hesitated after setting out to follow him. "Go ahead," I said, "don't worry about me," and watched her mount take her off into the night.

Chapter Ten

Someway I got to thinking about Plaza, who would have looked more at home in a bullring than dishing up meals for the likes of us. He didn't seem like the sort who'd conspire with rogues of Durphy's caliber. I'd been around long enough to imagine myself a pretty fair judge of character and hated to feel I'd been wrong about him. The brushoff he'd given me rankled. I wondered how much Johnson knew about him. The man did his work and kept his notions to himself. A hardbitten, taciturn hombre. Those intelligent eyes didn't miss much.

I wondered what he thought of us.

Johnson was still holding our outfit to a walk, which, in a way, rather surprised me. I had halfway expected, concealed in this dark, he would step up the pace, but he hadn't. Afraid, perhaps, we might run into malapais and break a few legs. It might be a long time but he had shown plain enough he had been here before. I guessed he knew what he was doing, though it seemed to me if we were to shake those redskins, night was the most likely time to be doing it.

We went on for a couple more hours this way while my impatience with the pace of our progress boiled into a downright suspicion of Johnson's maddening caution. What ailed the man anyway? There'd be damn little chance of cutting loose of those Paiutes once the sun got up to let them see what we were doing.

A rifle's sharp crack burst through the cadence of walking horses somewhere in the night up ahead of me and, jarred loose of my patience, I tore out of my assigned position and, afraid for Merrilee's safety, sent my mount barreling on up the line.

The whole column was in an uproar, horses rearing, flankers cursing as they tried to whip their charges back into line. Once past this squealing and whinnying pandemonium I could see the vague shapes of the girl and her foreman trying to control the panicked beasts. Johnson caught sight of me just as he got all four hoofs on the ground and gave me hell for leaving my position. "What's the matter with you?" he snarled in a temper. "Whole back end of the line could run away!"

"Are you all right?" I growled at Merrilee, whose trembling mount was now at a standstill. Her aggravated voice assured me that she was, and, shaken out of my accustomed calm, I demanded, "Who fired that shot?"

"We don't know," she said, "but it snatched Stovepipe's hat off—"

"An' damn lucky I was to git aholt of it!" he swore. "Fine shape I'd be in with no hat in this hellhole!"

"It was someone behind us," Merrilee explained, and Johnson said testily, "Some bastard tryin' to git rid of me, I reckon."

"Do you know where we're at?"

"Course I know—we're follerin' the base of them mountains north!"

"Then why are we dawdlin' along at this rate? With horses that could show a clean set of heels to those mongrel ponies them redskins are riding?"

"And that's what I want to know!" Merrilee said sharply.

It looked for a moment like the man wouldn't answer, then "Guess," he said, sounding confused, "I just sort of got into the habit."

"Then you better get out of it—pronto," I growled.

We went on then at the cavalry's pace of trot, walk, trot for possibly an hour, after which we put them into a hard lope and, from that, to a gallop till a grayness began to steal through the dark, and the early morning abruptly turned a deeper black and ten minutes later the rim of the sun crept over the high crags.

Looking over my shoulder, I could see no sign of the Paiutes behind us. "We've lost them!" cried Merrilee in great satisfaction.

"Hardly that," I said. "They'll pick up our tracks now the sun's getting up and be after us again without too much trouble unless we can find some hard rock to get onto," adding more soberly, "before they sight us."

"Then we'd better press on," she said anxiously.

Johnson nodded. "There's an old lava flow not too far ahead of us."

"How far do you reckon we've come?" I asked next.

"About twenty miles since we got onto this playa, this level footing."

I said, "Let's shake it up again."

"Not too fast," Johnson cautioned, "or the foals in this bunch are like to give out."

Curbing my impatience I set off at a trot, and this pace was picked up by the rest of our outfit. "Where's that Shoshone?" I·yelled at Johnson. "We should have caught him up long ago!"

Merrilee's foreman shrugged, not bothering to answer.

"I wonder," Merrilee said, bringing her mount nearer mine, "how many we've lost while you've been up here with nobody back there?"

Yes, I thought ruefully, you would think of that. But emulating Johnson I shrugged it off. If we'd lost a few, those Paiutes would find them—might help to slow them down a mite.

"There," Johnson growled, pointing, and up ahead, a-glint in the sunlight, I saw too late the frozen surface of that old lava flow. Too late because at that precise moment Merrilee, peering back over a shoulder, cried, "I'm afraid they've sighted us!" and we could see she was right.

Spread out behind, maybe three-four miles back, in a wide and straggling crescent came that horde of hard-to-shake Paiutes lashing their hard-run ponies.

Chapter Eleven

"What do we do now?" she asked, still looking back.

Johnson blew out a sigh. "Keep on," he grunted, dropping into a walk. "Ain't nothin' else we can do now they've spotted us. We can't run these broncs over this stuff."

"We going to lose all we've gained?"

"Not too much," he muttered hopefully. "When they git onto this lava they'll be slowed same as us."

Which was when Joe Lucie pelted up from behind. "We lost two packs when you went into that gallop!"

Johnson looked about ready to weep if you could picture his kind giving way to such folly. "Then we'll have to make do without 'em, I reckon. Git back where you belong."

Just another damned nail slammed into the coffin of what might have been, I told myself, glowering. I got to pondering then over the shot that had knocked Johnson's hat off. It simply had to be one of our crew, and somebody near enough to pick out his shape through the dust and the dark. I tried to recall who had been nearest to him. Either Red Durphy or that gunslinging Angel, I reckoned. It was just another of the perils we would have to put up with unless we could catch those damned rogues in the act. Everything seemed to be conspiring to defeat us.

Our outfit was moving like we were walking on eggs. Horses had a wild-eyed mistrust of this kind of footing. To those that were shod it was particularly tricky.

But we got over it at last, back into the crusty sand again, and stepped up our pace into the trot-and-walk pattern. The Paiutes had lopped about a mile off our lead but we'd recover this easily while they were still on that lava.

And we did—we even gained a little.

It was midmorning now with the air heating up, though we got some relief from the cooler air slatting down off the mountains. At my insistence we pushed them into a gallop for half an hour before dropping back into a ground-covering trot. This we continued for another half-hour. The Paiutes dropped behind till we could just barely make them out.

"Hell," Johnson said, "if we can keep this up we can git clean away from 'em."

Which was probably true had we been able to continue in this fashion, but we got into a stretch of rabbit brush and burr weed and were compelled to drop into a shuffling walk. The redskins I knew would have driven through this like it wasn't there, but with the foals and yearlings Merrilee was afraid we would lose too many. Put bluntly she didn't care to risk losing even one. And a short time later we were slowed even more and had to pick our way with care through a gopher village, where the ground was pocked with innumerable burrows.

We cut out of this soon as we were able but the headlong pace of the pursuit picked up some lost ground and we were in plain sight again before we were ready to hit up a lope. It was well past noon when we went back to the gallop. Those tough Indian ponies were hard to lose. But with a four-mile lead—if we could maintain it—I began to think once night came perhaps after all we could get away from them.

I believe we might have succeeded except that, just when it began to appear certain, a monstrous crack cut across our course at right angles, ten feet wide and some thirty feet deep, and instead of the slope one might have expected, both sides dropped sheer to the rock-strewn bed of some long-gone stream.

There was no possibility of jumping this. There was nothing we could do but race along beside it, hoping to find some place where we could cross. The Paiutes, quickly grasping our predicament, drove after us on a tangent that gobbled up our lead at an alarming pace. By the time we were at last safely able to cross they weren't but a short mile behind. And our horses, with all these frantic attempts to escape, were now too lathered to move out of a walk.

Fortunately for us the Indians' ponies were no better off. Both parties now moved at a shambling walk with night no more than an hour away. If we were able to keep going, the concealing darkness, once it enveloped us, might allow us, unnoticed, to turn off in some new direction. It was the only hope we had, and every one of us knew this.

Johnson, breaking a long silence, said, "I don't think Scotty's castle can be more than twenty miles from here. A bit more to the west if I can trust my memory. We'll turn off that way soon as we're sure those buggers can't see us."

The shadows stretched out across the dun sand reaching back toward the mountains, whose tops were still bright with the not-quite-gone sun. When we rode up a shallow trough that was beginning to tilt toward the distant foothills, the light became poorer as dusk began to close in around us.

But as though they sensed what we had up our sleeves those goddam redskins were lashing their ponies into a kind of lurching run. We could hardly believe it. I refused to, in fact, till I saw Joe Lucie clutch at his chest and fall out of the saddle with an arrow sticking out of him.

I'd have stopped if Johnson hadn't caught at my reins. "Don't be a fool," he growled. "That stick's through his lungs—ain't a thing you can do for him!"

I knew he couldn't last ten minutes but while I was hesitating, Plaza, coming up, whacked my mount across the rump and sent me pelting along with the rest of them into the thickening black ahead.

We were not able to make out with any detail our surroundings or what we were being chased into. Nights in the desert, except during storms, are seldom truly black; in their strange luminescence, while you might not see with any great clarity, you can certainly tell a man from a horse at up to sixty feet or so. This, I suppose, is because in the desert the stars seem bigger and closer. It was not at all likely we'd go crashing into any large rocks or towering buttes, but with those redskins breathing down our necks our greatest peril lay in being overtaken.

"If we get out of this," Plaza said as he passed me, "there's something I want to say to you."

Most likely, I thought, it will be something about Contrado or Durphy. If it meant another confrontation with them, the sooner we got down to it the better, I reckoned.

Back of us somewhere rifles were sporadically banging holes through the night but no blue whistlers whined past my ears; Indians, I'd heard, were notoriously poor shots, and of course right now they were firing blind, which was no guarantee you wouldn't be hit.

We didn't stop to fire back. I didn't think they'd have much lead to waste. It was the thought of arrows that bothered me most as we plowed along around rocks and through brush. Nothing but terror could have kept our mounts running. It came over me abruptly that we had changed direction, and the firing now was off to the right of us.

And now we were down to a shambling walk. Though I blessed the extraordinary courage and endurance of our horses, I knew they could not continue much longer. We would have to stop whether we wanted to or not.

On the heels of this conviction Stovepipe Johnson called a halt.

"Whether they come onto us or go on past we've got to rest these horses, no two ways about it," he declared. "I don't like it no better'n the rest of you but without these *caballos* we're not goin' to get out of this."

"We can't be far," Durphy said like he was Moses, "from the north end right now. All we got to do is—"

"Stay right here till these broncs is rested," Johnson informed him. "You think you can make it on a dead-beat horse, you go right ahead, boy, but them bangtails is stayin' right here till I say different."

Nobody had to explain to Merrilee what a fix we were in. It was amply apparent. There wasn't too much of the night still left, and once it was gone there'd be no place to hide. We'd turned west back there right after dark, hoping the Paiutes would keep going north. But out here on these flats the height of a horse would make him visible for miles. And how was our crew to stand off thirty determined and angry Indians with the prize in plain sight?

The end, you couldn't help thinking, was a foregone conclusion.

Chapter Twelve

We took care of the animals as best we could. There wasn't much to be done but sponge out their nostrils and let each of them have a mighty meager drink. Rest was what they needed more than anything.

There wasn't a heap we could do for ourselves either. Chew on some jerky and sprawl where we dropped.

I thought of poor Lucie back there where we'd left him. I hoped he was dead before those buggers came onto him.

Daylight still hadn't come when the sound of approaching hoofs presently got through to me. They didn't come on like a rumble of thunder, which was probably why I'd not been roused by them sooner. They seemed to be picking their way nearer with understandable caution.

I got the rifle off my saddle, made sure the muzzle wasn't plugged. And, like the others, awaited the inevitable alongside of Merrilee. I could think of no way we could shelter the horses. Played out like they were I saw no chance of them bolting. Stretched out on the sand, guns at the ready, we silently awaited whatever fate held in store for us.

A good many thoughts jumbled through my head, none of them helpful. Seemed to be taking them a lot longer to discover us than I had reckoned possible. Sure they'd no means of knowing with any exactness where we were, but to me they appeared to be almighty pokey. In another few minutes it would be light enough to see us. I guessed this was what they were waiting for, probably no more anxious to be shot at than we were.

Already the darkness was turning gray with day's approach. In this murky half-light twin buttes appeared some hundred yards off a little to the left of us, and just as these took shape in the dissolving shadows I realized the hoof sounds came from somewhere beyond them instead of, as expected, from the direction of our back trail.

Even as I stared in confusion the Paiutes, afoot, broke out of the clutch of fading shadows, and a spate of arrows swept across where we lay. Johnson's Sharps boomed instant answer, and one of those sprinting half-naked figures staggered back and went down. Then all of us were firing into that horde of yelling redskins. In the deafening racket of those Winchester repeaters the charge faltered, came apart, and as more Indians dropped, those still able incontinently fled. Only then did I realize it wasn't us who had turned them but the big-hatted hombres in cowpuncher rig sweeping past our position on hard-running horses through the smoky haze and reek of black powder.

Some of those renegade Indians escaped, but not very many. With the sun shining down on that scene of carnage we counted twenty-two redskins who had bit the dust. No survivors were in sight, and we had lost six of Merrilee's mares, killed in that first flight of arrows.

With the return of the unexpected horsebackers who'd so providentially come to our rescue, we began to sort out exactly what had happened. From Scotty's castle just before nightfall, the old prospector, having his evening lookabout through the old army telescope mounted in his tower, had seen a handful of riders with a large band of loose horses being pursued by a mob of mounted Indians. Six of this hombre's friends had happened to be present at the ranch helping eat up his grub, and these with three of his hands had caught up mounts and set off hellity-larrup to get a piece of the action. I suspected it had been nothing but a lark to that bunch.

"Well, that's how it was," the fellow said in his offhand way. "No need for thanks—we chipped in for the hell of it."

This Death Valley Scotty was a kind of celebrity throughout the West. Most folks—even if they hadn't met him—had heard at least some of the yarns being circulated about him. He was commonly believed to have a hidden mine someplace, which he occasionally visited to dig out a burro-load of ore whenever he happened to run short of cash. If you could believe the tales, he was nearly always pursued by a gold-hungry crowd of layabouts, more than a few of whom had left their bones in the drifting sands, invariably outwitted by the agile and desert-wise Scotty, who was said to have buried five-gallon cans of water from hell to breakfast, allowing him to keep going when the horses of his pursuers gave out from lack of moisture.

I'd heard some of the damndest stories about this ranny. Some people swore he didn't have a mine, that the fabulous ore he fetched into town had been highgraded. Others believed he had a rich backer who got a bang out of Scotty's exploits and had put up the cash for the castle this windy grandstander lived in. One thing about him was known by everyone: If you were broke, this bugger was always good for a touch, and you could generally find five to a dozen spongers living off him. Whatever, he was not a man to be taken lightly.

"Well," said Merrilee, "it was certainly mighty fortunate

for us you happened to be looking, and we're much more obliged than we're able to say."

I half expected her to offer him one of her best horses by way of appreciation. But she did not. We spent the rest of the day and that night at his place, and he certainly lived like a feudal baron, wining and dining us like a maharajah. I'd heard that for most of his life he had been a prospector. He had a fund of choice yarns he liked to tell about himself, of spectacular adventures and hair's-breadth escapes. And we listened to him and Johnson shoot the breeze at great length, recounting remembered experiences—true or not—far into the night.

We were all invited to stay on for a while and rest up our horses, but Merrilee was anxious to get on to Goldfield, and, by the time I was allowed to turn in, I'd had more than enough of this windy braggart, even though plied with a deal more whiskey than I cared for and surrounded by the splendor of Oriental rugs, vast oil paintings that sometimes ran the whole length of a wall, and other art objects too numerous to mention. Sitting around beneath fifty-foot ceilings made me near as uncomfortable as those windy whoppers he extolled with such charm.

Next morning Merrilee thanked him prettily but said we must go. We set forth right after breakfast, which was far from being as early as we'd have liked.

Walking our horses and considerably alert despite last night's tall-tale marathon we climbed out of Death Valley into the relative coolness of a high sage-covered range just as night was about to overtake us, and went into camp at a hidden spring Hungry Bill had dug out for us.

Several times that evening after grub I thought to catch our Spanish cook, Gil Plaza, eyeing me like he was minded to say something, but whatever it was he must have changed his mind.

Seven days later we got our first look at fabulous Goldfield.

A real metropolis by anybody's standard, Nevada's largest

city, with block after block of brick and stone buildings, hotels, restaurants, assayers' offices, a stock exchange, banks, livery stables, the famous Goldfield Club, saloons and dancehalls, plus one whole section devoted exclusively to soiled doves and their clients.

Johnson made arrangements for the care and safety of Merrilee's prized horses. The pack horses and saddle mounts we left at one of the numerous liveries. We all took rooms at the Esmeralda Hotel, situated at 211 North Main Street.

Several times during the remainder of our journey I'd caught Johnson staring at Plaza with a queer studying look like a man trying to lay hold of an elusive memory. Seemed sort of strange when they'd been rubbing elbows for more than the couple months I had been with this outfit. Whether Plaza had noticed this or not I didn't know. I hadn't seen the Spaniard returning Johnson's interest. The cook did his work without grumbling or complaint, taciturn and silent as a sack full of cats.

Johnson, too, had lately been more reticent. Whatever had been puzzling him was beginning to scratch at my own curiosity. I was not too surprised when on our second night in Goldfield there came a knock at my door and, opening it, I found myself staring into Gil Plaza's unrevealing countenance. "Yes?" I asked.

"Like a word with you."

"Come in," I said and, having done so, he shut the door and flipped the key in the lock, frostily smiling at my look of astonishment.

"Just making sure we're not disturbed."

"What's on your mind?"

"A number of things," he replied rather grimly. "These Rafter horses—what do you know about them?"

"Not much and care less except as their welfare affects Merrilee Manton."

"How'd you happen to sign on with this outfit?"

"What business is it of yours?"

"I'll be getting to that shortly."

"All right. I was hunting a job and was glad to get one."

Plaza nodded. "Understand you're from Texas. Ever hear of the Gourd and Vine?"

"Sure," I said. "Big outfit."

"I'm the owner."

"Sure," I grinned. "And I own the XIT. Come off it."

"Fact," he said. "I've been watching you, Boyano. It's my impression you're an honest man, so what are you doing with this bunch of prize rogues?"

"One could ask you the same."

"We'll be coming to that. First I'd like to pin down your purpose."

"If you think I'm hangin' round for those horses—"

"Then what's your interest?"

Maybe he did own the Gourd and Vine. The sharpness of his stare gave our cook a different look. The look of a man who was used to giving orders. "Only reason I'm here is Merrilee Manton."

Gil Plaza nodded. "I was afraid of that. Makes my position a little bit tougher. The start of her horses belonged to me."

"How's that?"

"Those horses Manton and Johnson brought out of Texas were stolen off my ranch."

It was my turn to stare. "You're accusin' her old man of bein' a horse thief?"

"No. I think he told Johnson what kind he was looking for, probably gave him a fistful of greenbacks to pay for them, and assumed the ones the bugger eventually showed up with were bought with the money he'd put into the man's hands."

"If you know this for fact, why didn't you swear out a warrant?"

"They were out of the country before I discovered the horses were missing."

"That's a pretty large mouthful to swallow," I said angrily, thinking of how this was going to hit Merrilee.

Gil Plaza nodded. "I suppose it is. I'd been off hunting cattle. When I got back to the ranch and found them gone it took a long while to pick up any trace of them. I must have run down a couple dozen rumors. Took me three years to get onto the right track; I couldn't devote all my time to it. Piecing together this and that I managed finally to get a description of a man who'd been seen with them—Johnson. It took more time finding a handle for him. Time I was able to connect him with Manton the both of them had vanished from most folks' memory. But I kept digging. I've spent as much in this search as I'm like to get out of them. These weren't young horses when Johnson took off with them; seemed pretty certain he'd latched onto them for breeding— my two best stallions and fourteen mares."

"So when finally you arrived at Rafter, the old man was dead, and you found Merrilee in charge. Why, if he was the thief, didn't you beat a confession out of Johnson?"

"Believe me, I wanted to. Situation I found wasn't what I'd expected—a bunch of damn rascals running the spread for a chit of a girl who couldn't possibly have been involved. Stolen horses five years older, about at the end of their productivity. I was about to approach her with the facts of the matter when I found out about that loan and the mortgage held by Beach and Bascomb. Then this Sneed showed up with his ultimatum and the girl with her mind set on smuggling them to Goldfield. What would you have done?"

"Don't know," I said, a lot of things that had puzzled me dropping into place. "What are you aimin' to do now we've got here?"

"I've been trying to sort that out."

"You must have seen what Contrado and Durphy had on their minds. What would you have done if they'd tried to cut out some of those bangtails?"

"Shot their damned heads off." A twisted grin puckered his tight-skinned face. "I was considering pushing for a showdown with Johnson when those Paiutes showed up."

"And now?"

"I'd be satisfied with half the increase."

"Expect you know she'll never agree to that."

"Can't tell—she might. Fair is fair. Probably go against the grain but I believe she'll come round."

"She's not responsible for your loss, you know. And if Johnson calls you a liar, what then?"

"When he knows who I am I think she and you will have no doubt about that," he said quietly.

"And here I been tellin' her he had her best interests at heart!"

"I don't say he hasn't. I expect there's a smidgen of good even in a horse thief. Fact remains Johnson stole them and pocketed Manton's money."

"Yeah," I said. "I suppose you're able to prove who you are?"

"No problem there."

"You want to have them in here an' thrash it out?"

"After all this time there's no rush about that. Let it rock along a spell."

"While you wait suppose she sells them?"

"I'll make sure that she don't until we have an understanding."

"What if I tip her off?" I asked, still trying to stay on top of my anger. "It's in my mind to do it, you know."

"Up to you. It won't change anything."

"No. But it will give her time to get used to it maybe."

"Maybe," he said, then showed me his twisted grin again. "We've both of us been had. I think she'll kick like a bay steer, Boyano."

"When she understands I believe she'll meet you halfway," I said hopefully. "What are you figurin' to do about Johnson?"

"That," he said grimly, "depends on Johnson."

Chapter Thirteen

After Plaza left I sat on the bed and stared at my fists seeking inspiration. Tugged two ways, unable to guess which might turn out the better. I was mighty reluctant to break this to Merrilee just when she figured she'd won out in spite of everything. Bound to be an awful jolt no matter how it was presented. Been better perhaps if she'd let the bank take them. But no, I reckoned not. This way at least she stood to save part of them with Plaza asking only half of the increase when he had every right to grab the lot. Now that I'd time to consider the facts of the business, it looked like the fellow was bending over backward to be decent about it.

And that foreman! I'd been right in the first place to regard him with an undecided mind. I couldn't think yet what had roused my suspicions; I'd been right, though, in believing in his loyalty to Merrilee. Probably, I reckoned, this was largely inspired by guilt over the way he had hoodwinked her father, stealing the horses and appropriating the money he'd been entrusted with to pay for them. If he *had* taken them, how would he react to the Spaniard's accusation? And what had Plaza in mind for him?

In the midst of these cogitations the door was flung open, and Merrilee came striding into the room, too agitated, apparently, to think about knocking. Burned brown by the weeks of broiling sun we'd come through, cheeks tight with whatever had put those bright flecks in her eyes, she rapped out in a temper, "Did you know both stallions are missing?"

I didn't, of course, being far less concerned with the animals than she was, but straight away the faces of Contrado and Durphy flashed into my mind. Shaking my head at her I said, "Are you sure?"

"I've just been over to the Union Feed Stables. Now I think back I don't know when I last saw them. When I was riding up there with Stovepipe I wouldn't have noticed. I'd hardly have seen them as one of the flankers . . ."

"Have you questioned Johnson?"

"I can't find him," she cried. "He isn't in his room, he wasn't at the livery! I had him paged in the bar—I'm half out of my mind!" she declared, and looked it.

A lot of wild thoughts leaped through my head. "Maybe he's off for a look at the town, hunting up old friends or talking to someone about your horses. Have you asked Plaza?"

She looked astonished. "What has Plaza got to do with it?"

"I don't know," I said, trying to think if this was the time to go into that with her. With so many things on my mind at the moment I didn't know what to say hardly.

Boot sound stopped outside the door, and Stovepipe's voice growled, "You in there, Boyano?"

"Come in," I called and, when he had done so, "What's on your mind?"

He was plainly put out to find Merrilee in my room and halfway embarrassed, a widened stare beneath his chin-strapped hat jumping from one to the other of us. "It'll keep," he muttered, and was fixing to back out when Merrilee caught hold of that hung-open vest.

"Did you know our two stallions are missing?"

He licked dry lips. "Well . . . you see . . . Matter of fact, I thought it best not to bring 'em."

"Not to—*you* thought! Why wasn't I consulted? You knew I planned to sell—"

"Wouldn't of brought much at their age. Didn't reckon they could make a trip rough as that was, Davy with that quarter crack we ain't been able to do much about an' Travis with that wire-cut knee. I couldn't help thinkin' they'd be better off at Rafter—"

"With that bank taking over and that hypocrite Sneed fairly drooling to get his hands on them!" She looked at him, furious, for once it seemed at a loss for words that would adequately convey the strength of her displeasure. "What else have you done I haven't been told about?"

Johnson shifted his weight from one foot to the other. At last he said, "I reckoned you'd prob'ly throw a fit is why I didn't tell you. I figured they was better alive with the bank than dead back there someplace in the desert."

She waved him away, too upset to go into the discussion any further. I guessed when he had gone I might as well tell her the rest of the things she could hold against Stovepipe. Not seeing any easy way to do it I gave it to her straight from the shoulder.

I said, "Gil Plaza was in here a while ago to say those horses your dad and Johnson fetched out of Texas were plain-out stolen from the Gourd and Vine. That he is the rightful owner, that he reckons your dad gave Stovepipe the money to buy up the sort Manton wanted and that Johnson, faced with such a temptation, simply stole the horses and pocketed the money."

I tell you I felt the worst kind of a brute as she fell back a step, all the color washed out of that bone-white face and eyes gone blank as holes burned in a blanket.

"Oh . . . Peep!" she cried, looking about to pass out as, with arms outflung, she lurched blindly into me, face pushed hard against my chest, every part of her shaking.

I was scared she was going to break down and bawl, and all I could do was keep patting her shoulder and inadequately mumble the way I'd do to a frightened bronc.

Then abruptly she stepped back, eyes wild with anger. "I don't believe it!"

"Don't believe what?"

"I can't believe Stovepipe Johnson, who had my father's trust all those years, could have stolen that money—they were as alike as two peas shelled from the same pod. He might have stolen the horses but I can't believe . . ."

"That he'd have kept the money that was supposed to have paid for them? Must have been," I said, "a terrible temptation finding himself with all that money and nothin' to stop him from stealing the horses. If they were out running loose on the range unguarded . . . That Gourd and Vine, from all I've heard, is the kind of spread it would take half a week to get from one side to the other."

"He doesn't look the kind of man—Plaza, I mean—that could own that big an outfit. And I certainly can't picture a man who could own an outfit that size turning up as a cook on a place the size of mine!"

"Put that way it does sound fishy. But you didn't hear Gil talking about it; way he told it carried conviction." Those eyes of hers showed an angry defiance.

She said, "And what's more I don't believe a Spaniard owns Gourd and Vine!"

"All I know is what he told me, and the way he told it sounded like gospel."

"What's he propose to do about it?"

"By what he told me all he's askin' for is half the increase."

She finally said with a hard-gained composure, "What are we going to do?"

Kind of set me up to be included in that "we." "Apparently," I said, "he's ready to write off his loss if you're willing to settle for half the increase, which has got to sound reasonable— maybe generous—when you consider what he's out of pocket and add onto that all he's been through catchin' up with Stovepipe. He's probably assembled enough proof to latch onto all the horses you've got. I think you better agree to his proposal."

It took a while but presently she nodded, though it was plain enough how reluctant she was. "I still don't believe he's a right to even one of them."

She wasn't thinking straight, of course, and small wonder, I thought, with all the jolts she'd absorbed . . . loss of her father, the strain of having the welfare of Rafter dumped onto her that way out of the blue, the strain of the last few weeks, and now this business of Johnson and Plaza.

I said, as I thought, reasonably, "If your foreman didn't keep the money, there was no point in stealing Gourd and Vine horses."

She threw out her hands. "I can't understand how he could do such a thing—robbing the man who trusted and paid him. And all this time you've been telling me Johnson has my best interests at heart! It looks like I was right in thinking some kind of change has come over him—"

"Look at it this way. Your father handed him a terrible temptation putting all that money in his hands to buy horses. What Johnson did is too low for description but against that I have to remember his unswerving, mule-stubborn loyalty to you. Wouldn't have been much trouble with the crew you've got to have run off with these bangtails any time these last weeks."

She shook her head. "I don't see how I can ever trust him again."

"If I stood in your boots, I'd not be in too much of a hurry to get rid of him."

"I expect Gil Plaza will be sending him to prison."

"Just have to wait and see, I guess."

Chapter Fourteen

Hard on the heels of that remark someone pounded on the door and when I pulled it open there was Gil Plaza with his tight-skinned face dragging off his old sweat-stained hat in deference to Merrilee. "Come in," I said, eyeing his bald head with its scanty fringe of gray hair. "Have you got hold of Johnson?"

"Not yet," he said with a questioning look.

"Yes," Merrilee said, "Peep's told me. I find it hard to think of a man I've been accustomed to regard as our cook really being the owner of the Gourd and Vine."

Plaza smiled dryly. "If you'd care to look over the papers in my wallet—"

She waved them away. "I accept your proposition. You may consider half the increase yours. Most of my share will have to be sold. Do you plan to sell yours?"

"I would certainly consider it, not being rightly fixed to get them back to Texas way things stand. Perhaps we could make some kind of arrangement . . ."

"You mean sell them as joint partners, each of us owning half?"

"I think, if that would be agreeable, ma'am, we might both of us come out a little ahead in that fashion. Would you prefer an auction or private sales? And will you take charge or shall I?"

"What's involved in an auction?"

"To be done up right an auction entails time, careful planning, sales catalogues, a well-known auctioneer, and considerable expense. One can make a bundle and just as quickly lose one's shirt. Selling privately can be handled by word of mouth or a couple full-page ads in the local papers."

Merrilee said, "I've already lost my shirt. I think we'd better sell privately and, since I fetched them here to do so, I believe I'd prefer to handle it myself."

Plaza bowed. "Very well. I'll leave the matter in your hands."

It crossed my mind the Spaniard, as owner of the Gourd and Vine, could almost certainly handle this deal with greater dispatch and profit, but I could see she had the bit in her teeth and, like Plaza, I decided to keep my thoughts to myself. As he was opening the door I said, "If you're off to hunt Johnson I'll go along with you."

Goldfield was a large and bustling place, I discovered. Even larger than I'd imagined. Two railroads had laid tracks into town, there were hacks for hire, and I was rapidly convinced the man I'd known as our cook was no stranger to the place. At the Goldfield Club he was boisterously hailed by several acquaintances who insisted on buying us drinks at the bar. Yes, he was here on business, Gil said; his associate, Miss Merrilee Manton, was offering racehorses at private treaty. Yes, he understood they could be seen at the Union Feed at Second and Crook.

"You mean John Diehl's place?"

Plaza nodded. When we got outside he said, "That ought to get the ball to rolling. Is Johnson a drinking man?"

"No idea."

"I imagine he'll down an occasional beer. Gold Nugget beer is brewed here."

We walked in and out of a couple dozen saloons without sighting Merrilee's foreman. "Well," Plaza said, "let's get a hack and try the livery stables."

We did. With no better luck. Not even at the Union Feed had he been seen since morning. The Rafter horses were being well cared for. Several Goldfield moguls, we were told, had been round to have a look at them. The owner of the Pipe Dream had seemed quite taken with a couple of the younger bangtails. "I understand," the proprietor said, "you're associated with Miss Manton in the ultimate disposal of these horses, Gil."

"I have a half-interest."

"Would you be interested—"

"Miss Manton," Plaza said, "is the one you should talk to."

We rode back to the Esmeralda and, stopping at the desk, discovered Johnson had just gone up to his room.

"Come on," the Spaniard said, and I stood at his side when he knocked on Stovepipe's door.

For several moments all remained quiet as the night before Christmas. Plaza thumped on the door again. Johnson's voice said, "Yes? Who is it?"

"Couple of old friends," the Gourd and Vine owner said.

But Johnson wasn't to be taken in that way. "Go away, Plaza. I've got nothing to say to you in private."

"Would you rather say it in front of the sheriff?"

Johnson jerked the door open with a gun in his fist, his countenance darkening on discovering me standing there. "Well, come in," he growled, moving back to let us pass.

Plaza heeled the door shut. "You can put up the pistol. I'm here for a talk."

Johnson looked at him warily. Somewhat reassured by my presence he thrust the .44 into his waistband. "So talk," he said gruffly. "Get it all off your chest."

"How much of that money you got from Manton can you still put your hands on?"

Johnson studied him, blackly scowling, whatever he thought hidden back of his stare.

He rasped a hand across his jaw. "You got a proposition, trot it out."

"I've spent a lot of time on this caper. Way things stand I've got you dead to rights, Johnson. I can put you away for the rest of your natural; you won't care for that, and it will do me no good. Couple years ago I'd have shot you on sight. I'm more interested now in cutting my losses. If you've enough of that money salted away there's an outside chance we can come to terms."

Johnson's face gave nothing away as he continued to study the Gourd and Vine owner. "Before I took those horses I'd never had a good look at you, which is why you were able to get on the payroll. Over the weeks you've been with us, a kind of vague disquiet began to work into me, but I still couldn't place you."

"All I want to know," Plaza said, "is how much you can pay to get off the hook."

"How much will it take to square things?"

"I want every nickel you can possibly pay. And a slow note for the rest of what those horses would have brought."

"So what would you have held them at?"

"You worked eight years for old man Manton. Two-three more for his daughter. I've checked you out pretty thoroughly. I don't think you've spent a hell of a lot in that time. For ten thousand dollars you get a bill of sale."

Good horses right now were easily worth three times what they were when Johnson took his gamble, so I figured, as Johnson must, the Gourd and Vine owner wasn't twisting the screws extra hard at ten thousand.

Johnson, apparently, was still turning it over. At last he said with considerable reluctance, "I kin pay you seven thousand. Might squeeze out another five hundred if you throw in the bill of sale." He said then, stubbornly, "And no damn note."

Plaza stood a while considering him. Abruptly he nodded. "Where is this money?"

"In a bank. I'll get you a cashier's check."

"All right. When you put a cashier's check for seventy-five hundred in my hand you get the bill of sale, and we'll consider the matter settled."

"Now," Plaza said after we'd left him, "we'll go *habla* again with Miss Manton."

So we went round to her room. When she saw who had knocked she regarded us quizzically but asked us in and invited us to sit down. Since there were only two chairs she sat on the bed. We put our hats on the floor, and the Spaniard said, "We've seen Johnson and come to a limited agreement. He's agreed to get me a cashier's check for seventy-five hundred, and I've agreed when he's done this to give him a bill of sale for those horses. I could have sold them at my place for ten thousand, so when you've disposed of the horses you want to sell, if you're willing to hand me twenty-five hundred we'll call it square."

She stared at him, astonished. "You mean," her voice got a little husky, "you'll not ask for any part of the increase?"

"That's right."

She looked at me and back at Plaza. Her eyes looked a little moist, I thought, as she regarded him with a bewildered expression. "I—I hardly know how to thank you . . ."

"No thanks are necessary."

"Such generosity . . . I never dreamed . . ."

"Fair is fair," Gil Plaza smiled. "None of this was your fault, and I'm glad we're able to settle it amicably. I don't believe Johnson ever intended to become a crook. The sight of all that money was just too much for him." He picked up his hat. "I'd be honored if you and Boyano would care to have dinner with me."

Chapter Fifteen

Plaza took us that evening to the Pearl Restaurant on which a gilt-lettered sign outside proclaimed:

> OLDEST RESTAURANT IN TOWN—YET EVER-NEW. SUCCESS IN EATING DOESN'T MEAN A CROWD, SUCCESS IN EATING MEANS CUSTOMERS SATISFIED. PRICES AS OF YORE. BOARD $35—SINGLE MEALS 50¢—HOME COOKING. 410 BROADWAY FORMERLY N. MAIN STREET. BETWEEN MINER'S AVENUE AND GOLD STREET.

Soon as we entered we were shown to a table. Tumblers of water were fetched straight away while the Gourd and Vine owner was making us acquainted with the friendly proprietor, Margarete Walter, who went out of her way to make us feel both welcome and appreciated. This was the cleanest restaurant I had ever set foot in.

The food was excellent, the servings generous. I could tell by the brightness of her eyes that Merrilee was delighted.

"I've never eaten anything like this soup," she declared. "It's positively delicious."

It really was. Oxtail soup—evidently a specialty of the house. Our meal was served in three courses, each better than the last. In the midst of her Irish cobbler Merrilee asked, "May one ask how you stumbled onto this place?"

Plaza smiled, lending him more the look of a Spanish grandee and large ranch owner. "I come up here a couple of times a year. As it happens, I've a small interest in one of the mines. When Billy Marsh and Harry Stimler, a couple of grubstaked single-blanket jackass prospectors made the discovery strike on a barren peak near Rabbit Springs, there was nothing this side of Tonopah but desolation. Initial assays ran scarcely more than twelve dollars a ton, yet half of Tonopah, where fifty-dollar-a-ton rock was being piled on the dumps, came over here in a wild stampede because Tonopah was silver, and this was gold," he said with a chuckle. "Gold will move mountains.

"What I started to say is that the first eating-place was opened in a tent by Stimler's sister, Lottie Nay. But the camp's first real *restaurant* was this one."

When he chose to abandon his customary reticence, Plaza, I thought, could be a fascinating talker. He went on to enthrall a big-eyed Merrilee with more stories of Goldfield's past and held her captivated for half an hour. It was a memorable occasion.

When we returned to our hotel it was just beginning to get dark and the stained-glass Rochester lamp hanging from the rafters threw a cozy glow across the comfortable lobby. All the rooms for guests were electrically lighted but the management apparently believed an old-fashioned touch in the reception area would give the customers a pleasant feeling of nostalgia, a longing for things far away and long ago.

As we came in, a couple of men stood up from their club chairs, threw a look at the clerk's grave nod, and moved forward to intercept us. Both wore range garb, and on the vest of the larger man I caught the glint of a badge. Stare fixed on Merrilee, he said without beating around any bushes, "Am I right in assuming I'm addressing Miss Manton?" When Merrilee with a startled look nodded, this badge-packer said, "I'm Bill Dorn, sheriff of this county. Are you the owner of that bunch of high-steppers being boarded at the Union Feed Stables?"

Merrilee's glance flew to me before saying with a touch of defiance, "What about them?"

I don't think this was lost on Dorn. "Isn't Rafter an Arizona brand?"

Merrilee, unable to hid her nervousness, nodded.

The sheriff, appearing increasingly grave, cleared his throat. "May I ask what road you came in by?"

She'd got hold of herself now and showed only a pretty bewilderment.

Dorn explained. "You fetched those horses from Arizona, I take it. By what road did you come into Nevada, ma'am?"

"Oh! We didn't come in by any road actually."

"I see," he said dourly. "Guess that explains why you weren't stopped at the border and why we'd no advance knowledge of your presence. We've a perfectly good road entering the state from Arizona. May one ask why you did not see fit to use it?"

"Guess I can answer that," Plaza said. "We came in from Death Valley."

The sheriff's brows went up. "Did you now? And why was this? And who are you?"

"I'm the Rafter cook," said the Spaniard coolly. "And—"

"I think I'd rather have the story from the owner," Dorn said dryly, cutting him off. "Well, Miss Manton? How did you happen to get into California?"

"We were chased there by Indians."

"What Indians?"

She said with her chin up, "I believe they were Paiutes."

"Paiutes, eh?"

He looked like he found this hard to believe. I said, "We were some miles southwest of Lathrop Wells when—"

"And who are you?"

"I'm one of the Rafter hands."

"One of the hands." Skewering me with the grimmest of looks, he turned back to confront Merrilee once more. "Miss Manton," he said, "did you bring those animals through Lathrop Wells?"

"No, we didn't—"

"Why not? Wouldn't that be your logical route?"

"We were told there was a large band of Indians there. Knowing the red man's love of good horses, we thought it safer to avoid—"

"I see. So when you were some miles southwest of Lathrop Wells, what happened?"

"A small band of these Paiutes raced their ponies several times around our column and then drew off. We went on, keeping a sharp lookout. Two days later as we were about to swing north again we discovered they were following us. When the sun came up next morning we discovered another bunch of Indians about a mile south of the original band—"

"Surely you had the heels of them?"

"We didn't care to run our horses, on account of the new foals."

Dorn nodded. "That seems reasonable. Then what happened?"

"We got into a stretch of malapais, and still another batch of Indians showed up off to the right of us forcing us into Daylight Pass. It was dark when we got there. By this time all three bands had converged. . . ."

"All told, how many Indians—"

"We counted thirty. We had hoped to stand them off in the Pass but gave up this notion. We didn't want a lot of dead horses on our hands. We pushed on through the Pass with the Paiutes still following about a couple miles back of us. Down on the Death Valley flats with night giving us cover, we pushed north along the base of the mountains, hoping to find some place we could hide."

"And did you?"

"No. Nor did we lose the Indians. Our horses were in a bad way. The Indians cut down our lead and just short of daylight—"

"Are you going to tell us these redskins attacked you?"

"I do tell you that. Six of our best mares were killed by arrows—"

"What happened to the Indians?"

"We prepared to defend ourselves."

"You opened fire on these Indians?"

"Only after they were about to overrun us. They crept up on foot but just when we expected to lose our lives as well as the horses, Scotty and some of his friends swept down from his castle. The Indians bolted. We spent the rest of that day and the following night as guests at Scotty's ranch and got back into Nevada the following noon."

The sheriff regarded us thoughtfully. "Did you come through Tonopah with these horses?"

"No. We headed straight for Goldfield."

Once again Dorn nodded. "Why at this point were you avoiding the roads? I'd have thought if you were still worried about redskins you'd have been anxious to get into Tonopah."

"It was Goldfield we'd set out for," she said simply. "We wanted to get there."

"Let's have a look at your health certificate."

"Health—" She looked at him blankly.

"For the horses," he said. "They've had blood tests, haven't they?"

"Why should they have had blood tests? There's nothing wrong with these animals."

"It's customary—in fact compulsory, when moving horses into another state. Let's see your health certificate, ma'am."

"I don't have one."

"And wasn't that why you were avoiding the roads?"

"Of course not! I told you why . . ."

The sheriff turned to the man who was with him. He was eyeing Merrilee with a vast disapproval. "My name's Kelleher. I'm state veterinarian. It's a considerable misdemeanor to bring horses into this state without a health certificate covering every one of them. Compounded in your case by not entering Nevada in a proper manner at a port of entry. You'll have a fine to pay, and you will not be allowed to move those horses till I've been over them and cleared the lot."

"But this is ridiculous!" Merrilee exploded.

"It may seem ridiculous to you, ma'am, but the people in charge of this sort of thing take an entirely different view of the matter. I'll warn John Diehl to make sure none of those animals leave his stables without my express permission."

He bowed stiffly, and without further words, departed the lobby and went into the street. "You can pay your fine at my office," Dorn told her, and followed the vet out into the night.

Chapter Sixteen

Merrilee looked to be having some difficulty adjusting to this latest in the chain of aggravations. She glowered at me indignantly. "A fine kettle of fish! How long do you think this will hold us up? A couple of days?"

When I told her I'd no idea, Gil Plaza opined, "Not over a couple of weeks most likely. We've put that fellow's nose out of joint. To even the score he'll be as officious as possible. The one most apt to give us real trouble is that sheriff. If he decides to dig into this, gets in touch with Tucson, and learns about that bank foreclosure, the fat could be in the fire for sure."

"By golly," I said, "let's hope *that* don't happen."

"If he makes any inquiries at all about Rafter . . . down there we'll be painted as horse thieves. We could wind up rotting in some two-bit jail."

Merrilee's chin came up. I saw the flash of her angry eyes. She understood now the full scope of what she'd got us into, but to say she was sorry or in the least bit penitent would be sheerest invention on my part. She was only furious at finding herself backed into this corner. It did not fit into her plans, and she hated it.

"What," she asked Plaza, "do you think we should do?"

"I don't think we ought to do anything right now. With luck they may be satisfied to slap a stiff fine on us, in which case I'll pay it. Be bad policy to rock the boat. If you're on good terms with the people upstairs a prayer or two would not do any harm."

I don't suppose she found this much consolation. Without saying goodnight she took herself up the stairs, and Plaza went off about some business of his own. I bought a cigar and fired up and sat down in the lobby to take another look at the fix we were in.

It was enough to cramp rats.

If that sheriff dug into the Rafter end of this—and he might very well—this could get awful sticky. Survivors from that Death Valley fracas, smarting from defeat, might also be fixing to kick up a row. There appeared no end to unpleasant possibilities.

Chomping on my gone-out stogie I tried to figure what might happen if we ran for it, but saw straight away that would only be digging us in even deeper. It was running that had dropped us into this in the first place. There was also Contrado and Red Durphy to be thought about and whatever intentions those two had up their sleeves.

Seemed I had cornered more worries than I knew what to do with. On top of everything else I felt an uneasy conviction a joker was hid out in this deal someplace, a strong hunch, you might call it, of something out of whack. Something I had heard, perhaps, that did not drop comfortably into the place it was intended. I knew from experience a good many hunches made no sense at all, but that didn't keep them from nagging a fellow.

I finally got up and tossed my smoke into the street. The more you tried to grasp a half-submerged memory the more elusive it became. Disgruntled, I dragged my spurs up the stairs, went into my room, and tried to will myself to sleep.

I spent a restless night. And Merrilee, apparently, when I saw her at breakfast, hadn't fared much better. The smile she gave me seemed to have come out of mothballs. Neither of us seemed able to dredge up much to say. After pushing the food around in her plate, looking up she said abruptly, "Let's go look at our horses."

At the Union Feed that state veterinarian, Kelleher, with two helpers in some kind of white coveralls, was conducting his examination. Far as I could see, about all the help he got from that pair you could have dropped in a pool and watched it sink without a ripple. They would lead out a horse and when he was done with it put it back where it came from. The presence of these three had attracted quite a batch of lookers-on.

The owner of the stables, John Diehl, came over when he saw us and expressed his sympathy. "A lot of officious tommyrot. Anyone can see there's nothing wrong with those horses. Understand you had a brush with some Injuns."

Merrilee nodded, withholding comment. He looked at me, and I said, "Chased us into Death Valley. Only ones we left there was Paiutes."

"And six dead mares," Merrilee said bitterly.

"That's a dawgone shame. Might one ask if you're willing to sell any of these horses, ma'am?"

"I might sell a few if the price is right."

"What kind of figure do you have in mind?"

"If you're interested, make an offer."

"You the breeder of record, ma'am?"

He fidgeted a bit under the weight of her stare. "What I mean to say is all these critters look like pedigreed stock—"

"What about it?"

"At the kind of price I expect you'd want, a feller'd want to know a bit about their background."

"It will be made available," she said, "to bona fide buyers."

"Could you give me a general idea of the breeding?"

"Top line on all these horses goes either to Steeldust or Traveler. Most of the fourteen original mares my father brought out of Texas were either by Zantanon, who was raced in Mexico, or by W. D. Waggoner's famous Yellow Jacket, which they'll tell you has never been beaten.

"As a matter of fact, he was beaten once that I know of. This was at Kyle, where a chestnut sorrel son of Traveler, with Jesse Parson up, pretty near ran away from him. And carrying more weight. This was a horse called King, who was later traded to an Arizona rancher for one hundred head of good half-thoroughbred range horses. King's new owner renamed him Possum."

Appearing considerably impressed, Diehl said, "I wonder if you'd step into my office a moment, ma'am?"

"Certainly," she told him. "Come along, Peep."

In Diehl's office, where we could talk in private, he motioned us to chairs and said, "What can you tell me about the sire and dam of that three-year-old in the fifth stall on the right out there?"

"Boy Blue is easily one of the best of the lot. He's a grandson of Traveler. You can't get any nearer than that; it's darn near impossible to get that close. When Dad came to Arizona five years ago he brought two stallions. An only son of Steeldust and an only son of Traveler."

"And how was this colt's dam bred?"

"By Zantanon out of a granddaughter of Old D. J., who sired most of the fast ones to come out of the Louisiana bayous."

"And what would it take to buy that horse?"

"I'm looking," Merrilee told him, "for a ranch up here."

"It'll have to have grass?"

"And water," she said. "Especially water. Either a year-round stream or two good wells with pumps attached."

"Happens I know of such a place. One hundred acres and not too much grass but with a creek that cuts round through the upper half of it—all the water you could use if you're figurin' to irrigate."

"Buildings?"

"Got a unpainted house five-six years old built of burnt adobes and three-four outbuildin's includin' a good-sized barn and another you could make into a bunkhouse for hands. Three round pole corrals, every joint anchored with rawhide."

"How long since the house has been lived in?"

"Less than a year. I got it off a widder woman who wanted to go back east."

"What's the matter with it?"

"Ain't nothin' the matter with it except it's on the far side of the mountain. You can have the place, deed an' all, for that colt."

"When could I see it?"

"Take you out this very afternoon if that would suit you."

Merrilee said, "I'll talk to my foreman. Let you know inside the next hour."

We found Stovepipe Johnson in the hotel lobby. He thought a hundred acres large enough if a pretty good share of them could be irrigated. So I went back to Diehl's place to say we'd go look at it right after lunch. He told me he'd feel privileged if we'd put on the nose bags with him—his treat, and I accepted.

Back at the Esmeralda we found Merrilee and Johnson still talking in the lobby.

"I'll go freshen up," smiled Merrilee. "Back in a moment."

Gil Plaza came in off the street while we were waiting. "I got off a wire to my bank," Johnson told him.

"Good," Plaza said. "I'll be glad to get this settled. Say when we can expect the transfer?"

"They thought most likely in about a week."

Plaza nodded and went on up the stairs.

When Merrilee came down and we left the hotel, Diehl hailed a hack and we all piled aboard. He told the driver,

"Take us to the Pearl," and outside the restaurant he paid the man off.

Inside we were treated in the same friendly manner as before, the proprietress appearing genuinely glad to see us. The place was more than half-full. Merrilee introduced Johnson as her foreman and said we were going with Mr. Diehl to inspect a small ranch property.

"I hope," Margarete Walter said with a smile, "you'll find it just what you're looking for. You're the kind of folks we like to have settle here. Good solid citizens."

I thought it pleasant to find ourselves described in this fashion and wondered how long we'd be giving this impression. After she'd gone off with our orders, our host wanted to talk some more about the Rafter horses.

While we were eating, Merrilee with a much better appetite than she'd seemed to have at breakfast, the proprietress stopped by our table again and Merrilee asked how long she'd been acquainted with Plaza.

"Well, it seems as though I'd known him forever. Let me see . . . must have been two or three years anyway—a real down-to-earth gentleman. And stories! He can really tell them. Has he told you about that woman whose son married a Mexican girl and was lost in a blizzard that very same night?"

Merrilee said she had not heard that one, and before Miss Walter could enlarge with more details Dirk Horba came bursting into the place with the angriest look I had yet seen on him. His eyes were snapping, and he said at full steam before he had halfway reached our table, "There's hell to pay!" and skewered John Diehl with his glowering look. "I've just come from your stables and that fool vet is givin' the sheriff fits. While him and his helpers was off feedin' their faces, the hostler was tied up an' gagged with a knot on his noggin and someone got off with six Rafter horses!"

Chapter Seventeen

Half the people in the place were on their feet but none of them quick out of chairs as we were. Dropping hard money alongside his plate, Diehl was first to reach the door with Johnson, Merrilee, and myself right at his heels. In less than ten seconds we were all in a hack with Horba outside on one of our sprinters pelting through town like a four-alarm fire.

Merrilee, I noticed, was too upset to lay out Horba, devoting all her adrenaline to pushing our driver into going ever faster to the peril of anyone not scurrying quick enough out of our way.

We reached Diehl's establishment in something under seven minutes, just about sufficient time for me to wonder how it happened that Horba had been left out of this snatch.

There was quite a crowd in front of the stables sounding like the gabble from a bunch of old hens as we piled out of the hack. The only persons attending to business appeared to be the state vet, Kelleher, and his two assistants, who paid no mind at all to these gesticulating citizens. Like Nero they went on with their thing whether school kept or not.

Plaza, according to Horba, had gone off with the sheriff and a couple of deputies to hunt down the horse thieves, looking truly deadly with that dark hat pulled aslant of his eyes and Johnson's buffalo gun in his fist.

"Well," Diehl said, after talking to his hostler, "there don't seem to be much we can do around here," having already looked to make sure Boy Blue was still in his stall. "I suggest we go on out to the ranch. Time we get back, Dorn will probably have captured both the thieves and the horses. That lanky deputy that looks like a sore-footed crane can track a scorpion across bare rock."

I had notions of my own about that but didn't voice them. At the long corral in the back of the place, Johnson and I roped our saddle mounts out of the remuda, including one for Merrilee, who was trying to discover which of her bangtails the thieves had got away with. When we rode back to the front of the stables she was waiting, still fuming, with Diehl, who was forking a claybank gelding with a big chest and haunches that looked built for endurance. She swung into the saddle of the horse we'd fetched her, and we all took off on the road round the mountain, that barren peak where Stimler and Marsh had found their first traces of color.

We passed Rabbit Springs, which Diehl pointed out to us, and before any great length of time was squandered arrived at the place he'd been telling us about.

It was exactly as he'd described it, and in less than an hour we knew almost as much about it as he did. Plenty of water rippling and gurgling in the length of that stream where it went through his property to where a few rods beyond it disappeared into the sage and sand of the desert. A few straggly pepper trees shaded the house and a dug tank was handy to the corrals. "Well, what do you think?" Diehl wanted to know.

Merrilee looked at Johnson, who nodded. When her eyes swung to me I said, "I expect we could make it do if you're satisfied."

"All right," she told Diehl, "if you'll sweeten the pot with twenty-five hundred the horse is yours."

Diehl said, shocked, "That's one hell of a sweetener! D'you know what this place is worth?"

"I know what it's worth to me," she said coolly, "and I know what that horse will fetch in hard cash."

"Don't reckon I need the horse that bad."

They considered each other like a couple of stray dogs. "That's up to you," said Merrilee, preparing to get back in the saddle. Her smile would have done credit to Simon Legree.

Johnson and I climbed aboard our mounts. The return trip was made with conversation in short supply.

Back at the stables, where we found the vet and his helpers still dawdling over their self-imposed task, Diehl said, "I'll have another look at that colt," and I reckoned the ranch was as good as ours.

Leaving Johnson there to keep an eye on Merrilee's interests, I rode back to the Esmeralda to look around for the other three members of the Rafter crew. As expected, I found nobody but Horba, who was in the bar. "Where's Plaza?" I asked him, and was told he guessed our cook was upstairs sampling the luxury of his room. No mention was made of Red Durphy and Contrado, and far as I was concerned none was needed.

I said, "Thought you told me Plaza went off with the sheriff to hunt horse thieves."

"That's right."

"Don't tell me they caught up with them."

"They caught 'em, all right," Horba said with his lip curled. "I told them two bunglers they'd never git away with it. Damn fools tried to shoot it out, and Plaza nailed both of 'em."

"Killed them, you mean?"

"Accordin' to that badge-packer. Two bangs an' them numbskulls was flatter than a last year's leaf!"

Gave me something to think about, a side to the Gourd and Vine owner I hadn't suspected. I'd known from the way he'd tracked Johnson down, the Spaniard had more than his share of stubborn determination, but after the way he'd got Stovepipe boxed and then turned around and let him off the hook I hadn't really figured him the killing kind. Still, it all added up when you considered the size of the spread he'd put together. He hadn't done that with no milk of human kindness.

Looking over my past I could see how I'd got to be a forty-a-month hand. Too easygoing for my own damn good. I just didn't have the real killer instinct, the kind of deep-down hardness it took to get ahead.

Blowing out my breath, I said to hell with it. Getting ahead wasn't everything. Until signing on with Rafter I had no trouble getting to sleep of a night.

When Merrilee and Johnson got back to the hotel I was still down in the lobby chomping on a stogie. "Reckon Diehl," I said, "is some put out."

Merrilee laughed. "I suppose so. He came around, though, before we left. I've got the deed to that place and the full twenty-five hundred."

I said, "You drove a hard bargain."

"How else do you get ahead in this world? He wanted the horse and, like Stovepipe said, there are plenty of ranches scattered through these hills. Bound to be one that would suit even better."

Johnson said, "We're short two more hands. It was Durphy and Contrado that took off with those horses."

"You got them back all right?"

"Sheriff brought them in just before we left. Where's Horba?"

"In the bar gettin' plastered, last I saw of him."

"Soon's that vet gets through wastin' our time," Johnson said, "we'll take the horses out to that place and move in."

"What you goin' to call it?" I asked Merrilee.

"Haven't got around to thinking up a name. You got any ideas?"

"How about callin' it High-Priced Horses?"

She looked at me blankly, then with reproach. "You think I overcharged him? Maybe you've forgotten I owe Gil Plaza twenty-five hundred. Whatever horses I sell have got to bring in all the traffic will bear. That ranch will take some fixing, and I've got payrolls to meet."

All true enough, I suppose. What got me, I guess, is that you wouldn't think to look at her she could be that grabby. Perhaps, were I in her shoes, I'd feel the same way.

I gave her a grin and fired up my chew.

After she'd gone upstairs Johnson said, "Now that we're rid of Durphy and Contrado it would suit me pretty well to get rid of Dirk Horba. I'd give odds that little devil was in with that pair."

"Think he got cold feet when it came to puttin' the rest of him where his mouth is?"

"Wouldn't surprise me. He's one of those hombres who'll butter you up while sharpening a knife for you. I get a damn odd feelin' every time he gets behind me."

"I've got him pegged for about ninety-percent bluff. He won't work any harder than he has to but I can't see him ever usin' one of those knives. Backed into a corner even a rat will fight."

He went off unconvinced to hunt for another hand or two.

I got up and pitched my soggy butt into the nearest spittoon just as Gil Plaza stepped in off the street. I said, "Those horses okay?"

"They didn't hurt 'em any. Just easin' them along or we'd never have caught up. You seen Miz Manton?"

"Gone up to her room."

"Guess it's time I scraped my face," he declared and went on up the stairs.

With nothing better to do I stepped into the bar, put a foot on the rail, and ordered a beer. That Gold Nugget brew wasn't half bad.

I tried again to latch onto that elusive something that kept making me feel like I was about to get clobbered, but it stood off and jeered at me just beyond reach. Seemed like it had to be something I'd heard, though it could, I supposed, be something I'd seen.

Disgusted, I went out to find me a hash house and quiet my stomach. I guessed I was getting more jumpy than Merrilee. She was looking much better now that those six bangtails were back in the stables and she'd got herself a ranch and that sackful of money she'd pried out of Diehl.

Chapter Eighteen

Johnson treated me to breakfast next morning, and it had me scratching around to think why till he said in a roundabout way, "Of all who left Rafter to come this far piece, the only ones left on the paysheet are you, me, and that sleazy Horba."

"Aren't you forgetting Plaza?"

"Last night he asked for his time and got it, too high in the instep to care to be seen with us common fry now we know he's the Gourd and Vine owner."

Site of this memorable occasion was the Mohawk Saloon at Main and Crook. The restaurant part of this establishment was pretty well filled when we came in. But Stovepipe, evidently a valued customer, was found a table within two minutes. They had a good short-order cook who knew his business. Nothing fancy but ample and adequate; more to the point they had our grub on the table before we'd emptied our first cup of coffee.

"He'll be heading for home any day now, I guess," I said, by way of keeping up my end of the conversation.

Stovepipe said, scowling, "Within the week I expect . . . soon as my obligation arrives," and tore into his steak as though it offended him. "Found us a couple new hands last night; one of 'em claims he can double as cook." He chewed a while then said, "Merrilee's hit on a name for that place. Goin' to call it the Pot and Hook; we'll be movin' the horses out there this mornin'."

"We going to have to rebrand them bangtails?"

"No. When they're big enough, she says, we can put the new brand on them foals that was dropped on the way up here—those that made it, that is. Meanwhile we're to start buildin' fences, we're puttin' chainlink up like we had at Rafter and dividin' the lower half into pastures. The wire, she says, will be there tomorrer."

"Seems like a lot of brand to slap on young pedigreed yearlings."

"That's just the name she fancies for the outfit. Pothook is what will go on the horses." He chewed some more and said, "Not much different than Rafter when you come right down to it." Presently he said, "Be harder to change."

On the way to Diehl's to pick up our stock, Merrilee said to me, "I've given Plaza that twenty-five hundred, and he's agreed if I can find buyers he'll not stand in the way of us making a few sales. Once Johnson's bank gets his funds transferred and he's paid Gil off, we can do as we please." She said with that clear direct stare of hers fixed on my face, "Tell me honestly what you think of that place."

"For the use you'll put it to I expect it'll do fine. Soon's you can afford it, if you figure to irrigate that lower half, you better bring in a crew of ditchdiggers because if you leave it to us it'll take half a year to get these pastures set up."

When we got to the Union Feed, that state veterinarian, Kelleher, put his foot down. "You're not moving these horses till we get through with our inspection and hand you a blanket health certificate."

"But you've already finished with pretty near half of them!" Merrilee protested.

"You heard what I said. Not one of them leaves till we're done with the lot."

Merrilee was furious but, getting her off to one side, I talked her out of saying any more. "You get that fellow riled we could be here till Christmas. We got plenty of work to do out there. This will give us a chance to get a good start on it."

So she finally subsided, and the new Pothook outfit rode out to their headquarters. We spent the rest of that day laying out the pastures, marking the lines where the fences would go, and she went back to town to try and work up some sales. Johnson cautioned her. "Don't approach anyone. Put an ad in the papers and let 'em come to you."

By the end of our second week in residence we had the fences all up and had begun laying out where the ditches would run. Meanwhile Merrilee had sold five Rafter horses, three four-year-olds and two a year younger. With the fence all paid for and money in the bank it began to look like we were a going concern.

Johnson had got his money and paid off his obligation to Gil Plaza.

Merrilee was back and forth between town and ranch getting the house fixed up to suit her and had taken care of the stiff fine imposed by the vet. Sheriff Dorn came out to look us over and to say we were free to move our horses any time we felt like it, and Merrilee said she would send in the boys to fetch them tomorrow.

The ditches were dug, gates put in, the pastures seeded, and the upper half fenced to hold the horses on the grass that was up there until the new grass was up in the lower pastures. The meanest job we'd had to do was getting rid of the cactus in which the place had abounded.

So bright and early next morning, the crew headed for town, myself with funds to settle our bills at the hotel and stables and pay the fees involved by that long-winded inspection imposed by the state veterinarian.

First off on arriving in town I paid our bill with John Diehl, paid the vet's fees and got our health certificate, left Johnson and the rest of the crew, and rode over to the Esmeralda, where Merrilee had not yet given up her room, and went with her key up to collect whatever she had left behind.

The bed was made, everything tidy. I found in the closet a sweater, a skirt, and a pair of Levi's, plus a box for a hat on the shelf above. Since the box was empty I folded the clothes and stuffed them into it, not caring to go out through the town carrying them loose for everyone to look at.

I was bending over to relock the room when something slammed into the door. There, just about where my back should have been had I not stooped, was a thundering great knife driven into the wood, as viciously vibrating as the tail of a rattler.

Letting go of the box, falling into a crouch, with a handful of gun I flung myself round, staring into the bone-white face of a man rooted in shock—the face of Dirk Horba with his eyes big as platters.

Chapter Nineteen

Shrill as a terrified woman Horba cried: "Don't shoot! Don't shoot! My God—*it's not what you think!* I never done it!"

Down the hall back of him a door was yanked open and Plaza's puzzled face peered out. "What's up?" he asked. Then, eyes swiveling to Horba, he said with curled lip, "Getting in some practice, eh? Always thought you'd come to a bad end." With this disparaging remark the ex-Rafter cook pulled his head back in and shut the door.

Staring at Horba, I was strongly minded to let him have it. Instead I told him to head for the stairs. "If you try to bolt I'll drill you like I would any other snake."

In the lobby I herded him into the manager's office. To the man's surprised look I said, "Call the sheriff—just tell him we've got a knife-thrower for him."

It didn't take Dorn very long to show up, and while we were waiting I sat with one hip on the manager's desk, gun still in hand. "This him?" Dorn asked, eyeing Horba grimly. "Why didn't you go ahead and shoot the bugger?"

"Wasn't sure my credit would be good enough here. Knife's in Miz Manton's door upstairs."

"You'll have to come along and sign a complaint."

I'd cooled off some by that time. "Guess no harm's been done," I grunted, looking thoughtfully at Horba. Horba said, still jittery, "Swear to God I never done it!"

"You were the only two-legged polecat in sight."

"I can't help it," he said shaking his head. "Honest, Peep, I never done it."

"I advise you to pull your freight," Dorn told him. "Don't let me see you round here again."

After they'd gone I told the manager I'd like Merrilee's bill and, after settling it, went back upstairs for the box I'd dropped, then left the hotel and got on my horse.

It had been a close call. I thought about it some more as I headed for the ranch, finally managing to put it out of mind. I didn't reckon we'd see Horba again. Johnson had got back with the new hands and the Rafter horses. I gave Merrilee the box and the receipted bills and what was left of the money she had given me.

"Did you see Horba? He wasn't with the boys when they brought back the horses."

So I told her about it. There was concern on her face. "No harm done," I said. "Funny thing. No one else was in sight yet I can't help wondering if maybe he wasn't tellin' the truth after all."

"You couldn't expect him to admit it."

"No. But the more I push it around the more inclined I am to believe him. He looked scared half to death when I spun round with that gun. Kept bleatin' he didn't do it. Seems now like the feller was too scairt to lie."

"But you said there was no one else in sight."

"Well, there wasn't. But the stairs weren't two jumps away. If Horba didn't throw that knife the one who did could have ducked out of sight soon's he let fly with it." I shook my head, still seeing Horba's shocked face. "Guess we'll never know one way or the other."

"We're well rid of him. He's been a grumbler long as we've had him, never half doing his work," she said.

"Speakin' of work I reckon Stovepipe can find some for me," I told her, and went out to look for him.

When I told Johnson he said, "Too bad you didn't clobber the bugger."

There was plenty of work for all hands getting the place the way Merrilee wanted it, tending the ditches and fetching up horses for visitors to look at. During the next two weeks we sold three more, two three-year-old colts and a filly. The filly was bought by some fellow for his teenage daughter. One colt was bought by the mogul who owned the Silver Pick mine. Nothing would do for the boss of the Pipe Dream but to have an even fancier one for himself. The third week of our occupancy two gamblers showed up, one taking a four-year-old for himself and the other buying two threes for match racing on the track they'd scraped out of the desert. No one paid as much as Merrilee had squeezed out of John Diehl, but she got good prices for all of them. The two gamblers were persuaded to cough up eleven thousand dollars between them.

At Merrilee's urging we finally got around to branding the yearlings. The Pothook had got to be a right busy place.

One morning when Johnson was laying out the work for us hands, he took me aside to say I'd better take the old wagon that had come with the place and drive in for some groceries cook wanted, flour, salt, sugar and canned goods, beans, salt pork, and a few other things. I stopped by the house to see if Merrilee wanted anything. She didn't but told me to charge whatever cook wanted, that she'd opened an account at the Main Street Grocery.

While the clerk was filling cook's order I walked over to the Mohawk Saloon and had me a mug of Gold Nugget draft beer, which slid down powerful easy.

Walking back toward the grocery I saw the sheriff stopping his horse to motion me over. "Been thinkin' of riding out to your place but now you're here it will save me the bother. Got somethin' I want passed on to Miz Manton."

"Reckon I'll have room with all these groceries?"

"Any room it takes up'll be in your head," Dorn said like he wondered if I could be trusted to deliver it. "After that business with Horba at the hotel I decided to have a talk with the manager. There was four of you Rafter people had rooms on that floor."

"Sure. Miz Manton, Plaza, Horba, and myself—what about it?"

"Kinda struck me as odd after all that denyin' Horba did that your cook's room was between them stairs and where you was standin' when that knife whacked into Miz Manton's door. Put a sorta bee in my bonnet, I guess.

"So I fired off a note to a sheriff I'm acquainted with down in that country askin' for a description of the feller what owns the Gourd and Vine. To make a long story short it didn't fit your cook. Not by a jugful. So I wrote again givin' him this Gil Plaza's description. What do you reckon he wrote back?"

"Ain't got a notion," I said, not mentioning what a churning I could feel in my stomach. "Go ahead an' dish it up."

"Well sir, he told me that description fit the Gourd and Vine cook, man by the name of Obediah Fenton. Been coosie for that outfit four-five years till he went off one night with Plaza's top stud."

I recollected in the light of these revelations the thing I hadn't been able to get a handle on, that elusive something that had plagued me for days. I realized now it was that remark the Walter woman had made about our Gil Plaza being such a great yarn spinner.

Dorn said, "It's my belief, Boyano, it was this fake Plaza chucked that Arkansas toothpick at you. Somethin' you done or said musta put his hackles up, made him think he'd better get rid of you before you let any cats outa the bag."

"I had the clue all right but it had sunk outa sight." I thought this Fenton must have been working on that hoax all the way up here from Rafter. No wonder I had pegged him for the taciturn sort. Reckon he'd been plumb busy smoothing up his story.

I said, "Pretty good talker once he put his mind to it."

Chapter Twenty

Back at the grocery I found our supplies all stowed in the wagon. My share of the work was getting up on the seat, picking up the reins, and clucking to the team. Put no strain on any part of me. What did keep me wakeful was the prospect of retailing those revelations to the folks back at Pothook.

Seemed like to me they'd be just as well off if they never found out.

Only trouble with that was the sheriff, not knowing they were still in the dark, would probably bring up the subject next time he saw them.

I didn't feel too bad about Johnson, figuring he had it coming after the way he'd done the Mantons, but Merrilee . . . well . . . I tried to sort out how I felt about her, which, to a ranny not what you'd call broken to harness, was no easy job.

Reckoned I oughtn't have been critical about her but it still kind of stuck in my gizzard about the way she'd run out on that bank and how she'd put the screws to John Diehl, knowing how bad he'd wanted Boy Blue. Still, in some ways I couldn't hardly blame her, left like she'd been with that flock of bills and a ranch to run after her old man had kicked off. She'd been strapped for two years, never knowing where her next meal was coming from, fighting continually to hang onto Rafter, feed all them horses and all. She'd been strapped when I'd got there and strapped when we'd left. And thinking about that, putting myself in her shoes, I could understand her acting like she had. I couldn't believe she was close-fisted by nature, and everything else about her suited me just fine.

She had real guts and was game as they come. As for face and figure she hadn't to take a back seat to anyone. Knowing how that fake Plaza had diddled her would sure give her a jolt, no two ways about that, but I guessed she'd get over it, probably soak someone else to make up for it.

About half the time on my way back to Pothook it was this Obediah Fenton that occupied my thinking. Slippery as calf slobbers and slick as an ice patch. And more damn gall than a herd of brass monkeys!

I didn't reckon we'd see any more of *him*.

When I pulled up in the yard at Pothook the first galoot I laid eyes on was Johnson. While he helped me unload and pack the stuff to the cookshack I told him what I'd found out about our bogus Plaza. He ripped out some language I'd never heard him use before, and none of it fit to print. Looked wild enough to grind railroad spikes between the bulge of them jaws. He was plumb furious there for going on ten minutes. Then, grabbing up a fifty-pound sack of flour in one big fist, he caught up a like weight of flour in the other and marched them into coosie's headquarters like they wasn't no heavier than a pair of goosequill pillows. In that kind of mood I thought it best to keep my mouth shut.

While we unloaded the rest of the stuff he simmered down some but with that black scowl still on his face he wanted to know if I'd told that to Merrilee. I said, "No. Not yet."

"Then don't," he growled. "She's had enough to put up with without being gnawed on by the likes of that bastard doin' her out of twenty-five hundred!" Then, straightening up, he said real soft, "I ever see that bugger again I'll kill him."

Knowing Merrilee to be sort of impulsive, and having a pretty good notion of Stovepipe's character, I couldn't imagine the self-proclaimed Plaza ever again showing up within miles of us. Whatever else the man was, he certainly wasn't a fool.

Things rocked along in the same old groove for the next several weeks with the horses filling out and the young ones frisking around like they knew mighty well they was something special.

"Sometimes," Merrilee said to me with that cool regard that could haul me up short, "you almost talk like an educated person."

"Yeah. I did get some schoolin' before I had sense enough to recognize the handicap. When I can keep my wits about me I do my best not to let it show. I got to live with these fellers and don't want them callin' me 'Your Highness' or something worse. The bunkhouse crowd don't much cotton to flossy ways and ten-dollar words. Gives 'em a feelin' they can't quite like. Top of that they prob'ly wouldn't know what I was talkin' about."

She laughed. "You're a hard one to fathom. I sometimes feel I don't know you at all."

"What's to know?"

"I expect there's plenty. You hardly ever say anything about your past . . . it's like you just fell out of the sky like that manna the pigeons dropped for the Israelites when Moses led them out of Egypt."

I had to grin at that comparison. "A forty-dollar-a-month hand can't afford a past, Miz Merrilee. Most folks—"

"But I'm not most folks. I'd like to know—"

"Some would call that pryin', ma'am. Around here a man is taken at face value until he proves different."

"Like our Gil Plaza, you mean?"

That brought my face around in a hurry. I couldn't read her expression but that remark sure left me hornswoggled. "Not sure I catch your meanin', ma'am—"

"I heard Stovepipe swearing like a mule skinner. I didn't make all the connections but I heard enough to know Gil must have done something you two didn't like. What was it?"

What could I say? I could pass the buck but the look she showed now told me she'd not be satisfied till she'd dragged it out of me. So I gave her the story I'd got from the sheriff.

She was riled, all right—riled plenty, but she came up with all flags flying.

"So he made fools of us! I suppose we deserved it, never thinking to check up on his credentials. I ought to have guessed the owner of a spread like the Gourd and Vine wouldn't hire out as cook to an outfit on the verge of going under." Then she said with her eyes suddenly flashing, "I'll just have to put up the price to the next horse lovers that come here expecting to buy racehorses for peanuts."

And that's just what she did. Some ranny that looked like a riverboat gambler in his black coat and tie and flowers embroidered all over his vest showed up the next week wanting a horse that could outrun a posse. She charged him five thousand and got it.

She doubled back to my past again after the sucker went off with his new horse.

"You know," she said, "what little you've mentioned only teases my curiosity. I'd like to know what you did before you signed on with Rafter."

"Don't you know it's considered bad manners to pry?"

"Not between us. Close as we are—"

"We're not close. You own this spread, and I'm just a hired hand. A man's entitled to some privacy, woman!"

118

"Not when he'd like to move into the house."

"Why . . ." I felt my face getting hot. "You ought to wash out your mouth!"

Her eyes were amused before, making out to be bashful, she lowered them demurely. "Back at Rafter I seem to remember you offered yourself as a way out of my predicament."

"Hell's fire!" I spluttered, "let's get the record straight. I asked, right enough, why you didn't marry yourself out of that bind you were in, and you gave me to understand you didn't know anyone you'd care to spend the rest of your life with. So, feeling—"

"Don't say you felt sorry for me. You said I knew *you*! If that wasn't putting your name in the pot—"

"There's considerable difference between marryin' a girl whose at her wits' end and one with a six-figure account at the bank!"

"True," she agreed with one of those blinding smiles I remembered, "but I've been thinking it over—your offer, I mean, so *naturally* I want to know more about you."

"What I recall is that when I spoke out of turn you changed the subject. So I figured, naturally, you were holding out for a better prospect."

"Well, I wasn't. I was flustered, that's all. Can't you tell, Peep, when a girl wants to know more about you she's *interested*?"

"I may not be as smart as Plaza but I've got enough wheels in my think-box to know a girl of your caliber is bound to want something different—"

"But you *are* different, Peep."

"Well," I growled, not looking at her, "I don't want to be."

"You mean you'd be content to spend the rest of your life just wasting away as someone's hired hand?" She hauled me around to get a look at my face. "You'll never make me believe it!"

"Look," I said, desperate. "Chinnin' with you is one of the joys of my life, but without you're fixin' to get me fired I'd better start doing some work around here." And, pulling away, I went stomping off to the chores laid out for me.

Chapter Twenty-One

It's one thing, I thought—a man's natural pleasure, to chase after a girl . . . but something quite different and strangely disturbing to discover one—desirable even as Merrilee—chasing you.

Some gents probably might enjoy such a switch; I couldn't think whether I did or not—I wasn't even sure she had chasing me in mind. She might only be pulling my leg, so to speak. Trying out her talent . . . way a man will fetch up a gelding to see if a mare will take the stud.

Which reminded me. With all these mares and fillies, what was she fixing to do for a stallion? I couldn't believe there was one in Nevada that could come up to her notions of a fitting and proper mate for her beauties.

I put it up to Johnson.

"Don't know," he said. "There's a feller over to Tonopah has a pretty fair line of horses. Sometimes a straight outcross turns out best—more vigor in the offspring. Got a horse he calls Rameses that's pretty well thought of. Don't know if she'd go for it." He rasped the back of a hand along his jaw. "Don't much like to talk with her 'bout such things—don't seem fittin'."

"If she's going to breed horses . . ."

"Oh, she knows what she's doin'. I don't question that. Old man Manton was as good a judge of horseflesh as any man in Arizona—you kin see what he produced. I believe she'll turn out good as he was. It's just that . . ."

"Yeah," I said, "I can see what you mean. Discussin' male animals with a young female . . . I'm glad it's you, not me, has to do it."

It was at this point that one of the two new hands came up to us looking about as bothered as I'd ever seen him. Johnson asked, "What's on your mind, Benny?"

"Somebody cut our fence last night."

Johnson stiffened, all attention. "What fence?"

Benny Crowder said, "Outside fence—up at that north pasture where we're holdin' the horses." He said, plainly puzzled, "Cut it up from the bottom 'bout two-thirds of the way, folded the lips back, then put 'em together with balin' wire."

"Show me," Johnson said, looking worried. "Any horses missing?"

"Funny thing," Crowder said as we headed for the day pen to get us some transportation, "when Dry Creek an' me made the count half an hour ago it come out right. Not short a one—so why was the fence cut?"

We rode up there. It was just as he'd said. The boundary fence had a slit in it that went from the ground pretty close to the top. Like an "A" without the cross bar, both sides of the slit appeared to have been folded back, then pulled together again and closed with three-four wraps of baling wire.

"Damndest thing I ever see," Johnson growled, wrinkling up his face. "Why would anyone do a thing like that?"

Crowder said, "To git at them horses is what we thought, but the count showed everyone of 'em's here."

I'd been eyeing the places where on each side of the cut the wire links had been bent and folded back. Johnson said, "They couldn't of got no grown horse through there."

"No," I said, "but with care they might have slipped a yearlin' through."

We looked for tracks but all sign had been brushed out. "Took more'n one man," Benny Crowder said, "to bend flaps in that wire an' bend 'em back again. Must of looked, when open, like the flaps to a teepee, but once she was closed it mighta been a couple weeks before anyone noticed. Look here," he said, pointing out bright scratches on several of the links, "there's where they anchored the cut ends to hold it open."

"I can't figure it," Stovepipe said. "If they come after yearlin's why didn't they grab a few?"

"Maybe they did," I muttered. "We better take a look outside this fence."

"The count showed nothin' missing," Benny insisted.

I looked at Stovepipe. "We could have the right count and still be robbed if they made a swap."

"You mean we got animals here that don't belong to us?"

"We get Merrilee up here we'll soon find out," Johnson snarled. "You, Benny. Go back to the house an' ask the boss to come up here."

Merrilee stared at the patched-up slit in our fence like she couldn't believe it. "What Peep thinks," Stovepipe said, "is someone's been in here makin' a swap. Has to be young stuff—foals or yearlin's. You want to look around?"

She was already looking. Benny said, "We could round them up an' run 'em through a chute. Be easier to tell—"

Merrilee shook her head. "Too much risk of breaking some legs. Youngsters are excitable."

She'd brought Dry Creek Folsom, our other hand, up here

with her. It was him who said, "We better do this afoot. We stirred 'em up enough counting."

Plenty of whinnying and a lot of high spirits accompanied our tour of inspection. "I can't see," Johnson muttered, "how anyone could move through this bunch in the dark and know what they were grabbin', let alone do it without these bangtails settin' up a clamor. They're makin' noise enough now!"

"They did it," Merrilee said. "That one's not ours. Those three foals over there don't belong to us. And over to the left of you, I never saw that roan yearling before—and look at that spindly-legged narrow-chested bay off by that tree and that dun that's got her head in the creek."

It took half the morning. Time we got through we'd counted six yearlings and five not over three months of age that had no business being inside our fence.

"What do we do now?" Benny asked.

Dry Creek said, "This is a job for the sheriff," and Merrilee said, "I'm afraid you're right. He may be able to find out who these belong to. Holding them in town someone may claim—"

Johnson said, "You think they're stolen?"

"Of course they're stolen. What I'm afraid of is the ones they took of ours in exchange may be out of the county—even out of the state before we get any action. Go after the sheriff, Benny. Get a wiggle on!"

Chapter Twenty-Two

While we were waiting for the sheriff's arrival Merrilee took Johnson and me over to the horse barn and the new-built stalls, where we were holding the four young stallions who were still entire. The oldest, a four-year-old, was a grandson of Zantanon, known south of the border as the Mexican Man O' War. This descendant of track-burners was about fifteen hands and some twelve hundred pounds, black as the ace of spades. The other three stallions, segregated in far-apart stalls, were dun, bay, and roan. The dun was a Steeldust on the top line. The other pair went to Traveler, one from a Steeldust dam and the other out of a daughter of Possum.

It was the black four-year-old grandson of Zantanon that Merrilee thought should be our top begetter. "We'll use the other three sparingly till we know what sort of progeny they'll throw."

Sheriff Dorn arrived with two of his deputies. By that time we'd corralled the visiting long and short yearlings. "Say!" Dorn commented, "you've done wonders with this place. Looks like a real workin' ranch now."

We took him and the two deputies up to have a look at what had been done to the fence. "Mmmm," Dorn said. "Pretty slick. No waste motion. You were lucky to spot it soon as you did. You looked around outside?"

"We figured it best to leave that to you fellers," Stovepipe said.

"Right. No sense puttin' new tracks on top of the old." He told the two deputies to go have a look.

Down at the yard again we showed Dorn the poor exchange we'd got for the youngsters that had been made off with. "Recognize any of 'em?" Johnson asked.

Dorn blew out a breath and shook his head. "We'll get them a good public place at one of the liveries. Obviously stolen. We'll put an ad in the papers. Prob'ly most of the owners'll show up to claim them. We have any left over we'll auction them off. In due course, of course."

The deputies came back, and the bigger one said, "Two fellers was the culprits. We found where they drove your stuff off. No tracks near the fence."

"Where do you reckon they're headed for?"

"Don't know. We follered along half a mile or so. Tracks pointed straight north."

"I'll round up a posse, take along a tracker, and see what we can discover," Dorn said, preparing to say goodbye to us. "Stovepipe," Merrilee said, "you go along with them."

So we let the swapped animals out of the corral, and the minions of the law, along with our foreman, went off with them on the road to town.

"Do you think," Merrilee asked me, "they'll have any luck running down our lost horses?"

"I wouldn't put too much hope in it. Guess Dry Creek and me better see to fixin' that fence a little better'n they left it."

"That black stud we were discussing isn't a grandson but an *own son* of Zantanon," she mentioned. "I looked up the papers while you were at the fence."

Dry Creek Folsom, being a local man, ought to know, I

figured, in what direction from Pothook the town of Tonopah lay. So I asked him.

"Straight north. Good road."

And Merrilee said, "You're not thinking of going to Tonopah, are you?"

"I sort of had it in mind. Fellow over there is in the business of raising a pretty fair line of horses, I'm told."

"That's right," Folsom said. "Name's Keach—Pers Keach."

"What sort of galoot is he?"

"Couldn't say. Never had no dealin's with him."

Merrilee asked if I thought our horses would wind up there. I shrugged and said probably not but that north, leaving here, was where they'd been headed. "If you're fixing to hide something, you could hardly do better than put it amongst a lot of like critters."

"Like putting a button in a button box? You might have the right idea. Go ahead. See what you can come up with."

"Goin' to be plumb dark time you git there," Dry Creek mentioned.

"Don't look for me back before late tomorrow," I told Merrilee, and Dry Creek advised, "Better pack you some water. That's a thirsty road an' not a grog shop on it."

As I headed for the day pen, he called after me, "Keep your Winchester handy."

It was a sure enough lonesome road and drifted over in places traveling through that desert. It was lucky I had a good sense of direction or I could have found myself going around in circles. I didn't see any dunes but sand was piled up wherever there was bushes. I didn't see any cows—no pilgrims, either.

When I got into Tonopah where it sat among low hills it must have been pretty late but lights were still showing;

plenty of people, too, most of them under wide brims whose crowns were creased like cavalry hats. Not a single curled brim did I spot, not even a derby until I stepped into a saloon to wet my whistle. Some woman crossed the dusty street just ahead of me packing a furled umbrella in a town that didn't look like it had ever seen rain.

I came out of the saloon and took a quick look around, hunting a place to lay my head. I discovered the Butler Meat Market wedged in among a number of other mighty narrow storefronts with wooden awnings over plank walks, and farther down the road Jerry Ahern's General Merchandise. Three doors closer I found White's Hotel. Most of the buildings in sight had two stories, at least a couple had three.

I went into White's and signed for a room, paying in advance as instructed, and went out then to find a place for my horse.

A covered wagon went by, the owner walking alongside it, his four teams on a jerkline and bound out of town, fixed to do his moving in the cool of the night.

When I got myself up next morning, not having noticed any eateries, I stopped at the desk and the day clerk told me where I might find one. "You stayin' over?"

"Don't expect to. I'm from Goldfield. Where'll I find Pers Keach and his horses?"

"At this time of day he ought to be to home," he said, and gave me directions for finding Keach's place.

After eating my breakfast, which was nothing to brag about, I picked up my horse and made a tour of the liveries and boarding corrals without seeing any of the missing Pothook youngsters.

Must have been going on nine when I got to Keach's place, some two miles out of town. He had a dug well and a tank and five fair-sized corrals in the shade of several old cottonwoods and a house that had never known a lick of paint or much care either. His barn, however, made over into stables, was fancied up with both paint and gingerbread scrolls and curlicues.

He was big, was Keach, a regular hogshead of a man, with side whiskers, chin whiskers, and hair on the backs of both hands. He had a toothpick sticking out of his mouth that bobbed up and down with most of his talk coming out from around it. He had a voice like an organ and mean little eyes that took me in from head to foot.

"You lookin' to buy a horse?"

"Depends. Let's just say I'm lookin'."

"Couldn't have come to a better place. What did you have in mind?"

"A good one."

"How high did you figger to go, friend?"

"What I'm lookin' for is breeding stock."

"Mares, you mean?" He was still looking me over in a disparaging way.

"Stud," I said, "if you've got one looks good enough."

"Don't believe I caught your name."

Those mean little eyes had brightened considerably. They narrowed craftily when I said, "Don't believe you did. We goin' to chin all day? If you've got what I'm after let's have a look at him."

"Right this way, friend. You'd have to be dang hard to suit not to like this critter," he declared, heading for the barn. There was a lot of whinnying when we stepped into it. What windows the place had were pretty high up but I could see well enough when he led out a bay stallion that had a knob on one knee. "Too old," I said.

He put the horse back in its stall and led out another, a dun this time. I shook my head. "I'm lookin' for something that'll throw more speed."

"Why the hell didn't you say so?" He put the dun back and, crossing to the barn's far side, led out a sorrel with flax mane and tail whose lines suggested he might have run some when younger.

"That the best you can do?"

"This stud is worth every nickel I'm askin'."

"Not to me," I said, heading for the doors.

"Hold on," he growled. "You wouldn't be interested in a young horse, would you?"

"How young?"

"Too young for service, but he'll grow out of it. Make a damn fine stallion one of these days. Has the look of a sure-enough track burner—a real speed merchant is what he looks like to me."

"Who's he by? What's he out of?"

"Don't know. I bought him off a feller goin' through with a bunch of horses."

"I guess not," I said, turning away.

"By Gawd, you can't fault this'un!" he muttered, and fetched out a long yearling that was roan in color and built like a dream. Keach walked him around for me, showing him off.

"You got a bill of sale for him?"

"Course I've got a bill o' sale for him!" He gave me a hard look. "Don't think I'd chance gettin' stuck with a stole horse, do you?"

"How much you askin'?"

"One thousan' bucks, an' cheap at the price."

He was right about that. The colt was one of ours.

"I'll think about it. I'll probably be around for a couple of days—"

"If you like him you'd better latch onto him right now!"

He was beginning to look ugly. I could read suspicion in those mean little eyes. He said, "That colt'll likely go the next time I show him."

"Yeah, they all tell me that. I'd like him better if he was a couple years older. For a horse so young that's a pretty stiff price."

"Stiff, hell! At what I'm askin' that horse is a steal!"

"Well, I'll think about it. If I make up my mind—"

"You better make it up quick if you want him."

I went on out and got into the saddle and set off for town. I could feel that bugger's eyes boring into me, but didn't look back.

Soon as I got in town I asked for the sheriff. "Sheriff's down to Goldfield. All we've got is a deputy here."

"I'm in kind of a hurry—where'll I find him?"

He told me. I found him. I said, "There's a stolen high-priced yearling stud on up the road a piece—long yearlin' actually. Taken from a ranch north of Goldfield along with ten others couple of nights ago."

"Yeah? You talkin' about Keach?"

I nodded.

"What you want me to do about it? You accusin' Keach of stealin' it?"

"No. What I want you to do is pick up the colt and keep him in a safe place till I can get some folks over here to identify it. Keach claims he bought it, and he probably did. I'd like for you to go through his place and see if any of the others are there. I'll go along with you."

He'd been looking me over. "Be right with you," he said, went out back of the office, and came back in the saddle on a big powerful *grulla*.

"You got a handle?"

"Name's Boyano. Work for the outfit that lost these youngsters. Pothook."

"Place that woman's runnin'?"

"That's right."

"You acquainted with Dorn?"

I nodded. "Sheriff's out huntin' these *caballos* right now," I said. "We figure there was two of them. We got chainlink. We found where they cut the wire. Real cute job. Cut the wire, bent it back, led them youngsters through, and refastened the slit."

We rode into Keach's yard and got down. Deputy said when Keach came out of the barn, "You try to sell this feller a horse?"

Keach gave me an ugly look. "What of it?"

"Let's have a look at that animal."

Keach hung fire for a bit like he was minded to say it was sold and gone. But looking at my face I guess he thought better of it. "In the barn," he said, and led us to the stall.

"Didn't you guess this horse was stolen?"

"Who says?"

Deputy jerked his chin at me. "This feller."

"If the horse was stolen, I paid too much for him."

"He was stolen, all right. Two nights ago from the Pothook north of Goldfield," I said. Deputy said, "He ought to know. Says he works for 'em."

"Then I'm out a pile of money," Keach snarled.

"Tough," said the deputy. "Oughta be more careful who you buy horses from. I'll be takin' him along. Right now I'll look at the rest of your horses."

Keach shot a murderous look at me, but put up no argument.

We didn't find any others. Deputy said to Keach, "Let's have a halter with a shank fastened onto it. You can pick it up at my office."

We didn't ask to see his bill of sale. The fellow wouldn't hardly have put his own name on it. Deputy wanted to know what the man looked like.

The description Keach gave us didn't mean a damn thing. It would have fit half the men in the state.

Chapter Twenty-Three

Taking it easy in the heat of the day, I got back to Pothook just in time for supper. Merrilee came out as I was putting my horse in the day pen. "No luck, I suppose—did you find out anything?"

"That Keach hombre tried to sell me that roan for a thousand. Had the Tonopah deputy pick him up. We looked around some but couldn't find any more. Keach claims he bought him off some fellow goin' through with a bunch of horses. I expect he bought him. For less than half what he's askin' probably. I told the deputy some folks would be over to identify the colt. Maybe you and Stovepipe ought to go over there tomorrow."

"You did first rate. Stovepipe hasn't got back yet. If they don't lose the tracks perhaps they'll come up with the others."

"Yeah. Maybe," I said.

"You don't think so."

"I don't think they'll risk selling any more this close, is all. Trackin' slick crooks in this kind of country ain't easy as fallin' off no log. When I signed on, how long," I said, "had Horba been at Rafter?"

"About two weeks." She gave me a shrewd and searching look. "What has Horba to do with this discussion?"

"Thought I saw him when I was in Tonopah. Don't seem too likely. It was only for the quick half of a second. Some trick of the light most probably."

It put a thoughtful twist to Merrilee's expression. "I hope he's not still hanging around."

I hoped not, too. If Horba was here and hooked up with Keach . . . That prospect did not appeal to me at all. Horba knew too much about the way we did things, our likeliest thoughts and reactions. And I wondered again which of them had flung that knife, him or Plaza-nee-Fenton.

If Horba had taken up with Keach we could be in bad trouble—worse than it looked like. That little rat knew Johnson's habits. And mine. He could easily guess the best time and place to hit us hardest. As someone already had—two someones according to those deputies who'd sorted out the tracks.

Stovepipe Johnson returned the next morning from his tour with Dorn's posse. Had a discouraging look of frustration about him. Tracks of the stolen youngsters had led them on an exasperating chase and had not—he said when questioned—taken them anywhere close to Tonopah before vanishing completely.

Next day after Johnson's return he and Merrilee went over there and brought back the roan colt. Which left the other ten colts, geldings, and fillies yet to be accounted for—still, I thought, to be fed into Keach's operation one at a time whenever it looked feasible.

The Tonopah deputy had promised to keep an eye on Keach's place, but I put no great amount of hope into that. He had too many other chores to see to.

Two more weeks went by with no further word from him. Our days at Pothook were occupied with the routine tasks of a working horse ranch. All but two of the young horses left with Dorn to dispose of had been claimed by their shoestring owners. Each night one or another of us three Pothook hands were told by Johnson to ride our outside fence in the rather forlorn hope of preventing further losses. Never having been especially bright about number facts, I had not figured the exact mileage represented by a fence surrounding one hundred acres, some of them hilly. There was no place at Pothook from which all sections of this fence could be seen—not even with a glass. And the constant need to stay on our toes began to wear on us and shorten our tempers. Little irritations we wouldn't normally have noticed soon began to assume an unhealthy magnitude, making mountains out of molehills.

Gopher hills, actually. For there was one section of that big northern pasture that had become a regular gopher community. They were hard to discourage, nearly impossible to stamp out. Putting poison down their burrows got a lot of them but not all, and Merrilee hated to have us do it, but hated even worse to have us shoot horses with broken legs.

During this period we had sold three more of her adult prancers, a three-year-old gelded colt and two four-year-old mares. She had about reached the point of making up her mind to keep what was left.

In a lot of ways I suppose you might say, being opposites in character traits, Merrilee and myself sort of complemented each other. She was impulsive—a spur-of-the-moment kind of person, where generally I was more inclined to be the careful sort, wanting to get a handle on a thing before making a decision. She was frugal yet apt to be acquisitive where I was more easy-going, harder to upset, and rather more likely to put things off—a part, no doubt, of my Mexican heritage, the manyanner syndrome gringos cuss and kid about.

In any event we got along like two six-shooters in the same belt. Oh, we bickered some and upon occasion irritated each other but we weren't either of us the sort to nurse a grudge. Despite my lackadaisical nature I guess Keach and Horba were a great deal more on my mind than they were on hers. Once a thing was past she was inclined to forget it, save where it represented a direct loss to her pocketbook.

In my own mind I'd written off those young horses someone had sifted through the fence. I felt reasonably sure they were gone for good. If Keach had been mixed up in it, he would be doubly cautious of being caught with another one on his property.

As any old bush-track match-race man could tell you, there were plenty of ways a horse could be disguised or made to look like another even-better-known animal. Those youngsters we'd lost could still be around here. Being fully aware of this and without honestly expecting to see any of them again, I did keep my eyes open, and one day, astonished, I was pretty sure I'd seen one.

I had gone into town with the wagon at cook's behest to fetch back some more of the truck he needed in his kitchen, flour and sugar and a variety of tinned stuff. At Dry Creek's urging I had driven around to Sheck & Company's emporium at 112 East Crook where, according to him, we could get better prices than we'd been enjoying at the Main Street Grocery.

I had just come out with my arms full when some ranny rode past with a blaze-faced filly on a leadshank. Something about the way this animal moved caught at my attention. She was well set up, a zebra dun with intelligent eyes and a fine way of going with speed in every line, and I stood staring after them, wondering at her being with such a seedy down-at-heels character.

We had lost a zebra dun short two-year-old to those fence cutters that would now be just about her size, I figured. It was the blazed face and cropped mane and tail that put me off. I put my groceries in the wagon and went back to get the rest of cook's order.

"You see that fellow that just went past with that filly on lead?" I asked the storekeeper.

"Sure. Lem Tucker. Got a place south of here. Sort of fancies himself as a racehorse man. Doubt he'll ever amount to much—owes everybody fool enough to give him credit."

"Where'd he get hold of that dun filly?"

"No idea. Raised her, I guess."

I took the rest of our stuff out, stepped onto the hub, and settled into the seat, still thinking about that dun filly of Tucker's. We don't crop manes and tails at Pothook, and the dun we had lost didn't have a blazed face, but I guessed a good bleach could probably take care of that. She looked thinner than ours, her hoofs were rough, and she was bad in need of a currycomb, but she stuck in my mind all the way home.

I unloaded the groceries, put up the horse and wagon, and went across to the house, and when Merrilee came and held the screen open with a smile that was almost bright as the day I said, "Think I saw that dun filly we lost."

"Where?" she said, letting go of the smile with her eyes concerned. "In town?"

"Just as I was comin' out of the grocery this seedy-looking character went by with this dun on a leadshank. Way she moved reminded me of yours. Heap thinner than I remembered, hoofs needed attention, mane and tail cropped and a wide blaze on her face. Storekeeper said the fellow leadin' her was Lem Tucker, said Lem fancies himself as a racehorse man."

"The dun filly we lost didn't have a blazed face."

I nodded. "Just the same I'd give odds that filly was one of yours."

"Find out where this Tucker can be reached."

"Got a place south of town. Out there in the rabbit brush is what it sounded like. Why don't you get the sheriff to go out there with you?"

"We don't need Dorn—not yet anyway. Saddle old Queeny and a horse for yourself, and we'll go take a look. If she's ours she's the dun Queeny dropped two years ago."

So half an hour later we took the Goldfield road. Merrilee was looking pretty animated. I cautioned her not to get her hopes too high. "Probably wishful thinking on my part," I said. "Man would be a fool to risk showing a stolen horse this close to home."

"He might not know she was stolen—"

"If he put that blaze on her face he knows."

Also, I thought, if he did use bleach he'll have to keep using it as the hair grows out. Long as he stays in these parts, anyway. If he had a lick of sense he wouldn't keep her round here, not if she's ours and he knows she was stolen.

When we reached Goldfield we took the road south, watching both sides and taking a sharp look wherever we saw horses because, after all, some of those others might be around here.

"How far south?"

"Don't know," I said. "Didn't think to ask."

Next place we came to, Merrilee, turning off the road, swung Queeny into the yard. A woman came to the door, and Merrilee explained who we were hunting. "About a mile further south on the lefthand side," the woman said. "Boxed T."

A damn dilapidated-looking place, I thought, when we got there. Everything held together with baling wire—even the whoppyjawed corral with three horses in it, one of them the dun. Both she and Queeny began whickering. Tucker bulged out of a thrown-back door, took one look, and went for his iron.

His first shot missed by inches. Mine did better. He fell back against the doorjamb, and with his back still against it sprawled half off the top step.

Merrilee stared from a gone-white face. "Hadn't we better do something about him?"

"Bit late for that," I said, looking around. "He's halfway there already. If he's got any help they're keeping out of sight."

"Halfway where?"

"Wherever they take dead horse thieves," I growled. "We're goin' to have to see Dorn about this, I reckon. There's a halter and shank on that top rail. Go put it on your filly and lead her out while I watch the door."

But nothing more happened. No one showed up. I put the bars up again, and we headed for town.

Chapter Twenty-Four

The sheriff listened intently as I filled him in on what had happened at the Boxed T. "Are you sure Tucker's dead?" he asked when I'd finished.

"I expect he is. You'll be wanting to have a look at him, anyway, and do something about the two horses we left in his corral. Didn't seem to be nobody else around."

"No, he lived by himself. I'll send a deputy down to take care of it. Glad you got your filly back, Miz Manton."

She tried to dredge up a smile, but it didn't have the zing she usually put into them. I guess she was still seeing Tucker sliding down that doorjamb. I nodded to Dorn, and we headed for home, neither of us being in the mood for small talk.

"Well!" Johnson said when we turned into the yard. "What you got there? Looks like Queeny's two-year-old except for the face."

"It is," Merrilee said, and went on into the house.

"What's ailin' her?"

"She watched me kill a man," I said and told him about it. Johnson clucked. "You reckon he was mixed up in it?"

I shrugged. "He had the filly and obviously knew she was stolen or he'd not have come out of there grabbin' for iron. Can't see him bein' either of the two Dorn's deputies mentioned. Not bright enough," I said.

He nodded. "They was right about that. Only two shod horses in the tracks we follered." He gave me a speaking look. "She oughta get the whole bunch shod."

"Yeah. With some kind of mark. Make them easier to follow."

"I know just the man we oughta have for the job—oughta have him anyhow. Nels McGee. Old racehorse man. What that feller don't know about bangtails ain't worth knowin'."

"She can afford it. Better see if you can get him. Local man, is he?"

"Drifts around. Come from up north someplace."

"I'll speak to her about him . . . You better do it. You're the cock-a-doodle-doo around here."

He did. And she agreed. And a couple days later the new man arrived, and we set up a forge shop and he got busy.

This McGee was no spring chicken. You might have thought him a deacon or some other church functionary, going by his garb. Low-crowned hat, forktailed coat, apparently worn rain or shine, striped pants—every stitch about him a sort of rusty black. He was seamed and wrinkled as a Kansas prune. Angular and wiry, must have been well into his middle sixties, a sandy-haired hombre who gave Dakota as his starting place. And knew more about prancers, according to Stovepipe, than they knew about themselves.

"You got some nice horses here," he told us. Merrilee was quite impressed with him. "Certainly seems to know what he's doing," she said. And Johnson said, "With him around you kin forget about vets. Got anything they'll need right there in that carpetbag."

A few days after this new fellow's advent, Merrilee

beckoned me over to where she was sitting on the porch buffing her nails. "You know," she commenced, "I believe that pair that got away with our horses may be someone we know or have seen before."

"What gives you that notion?"

"I don't know, but that's what I think. Someone who's been around here."

"Like Horba?"

"Seems possible, doesn't it? Or someone maybe who has bought a horse or two from us."

"It's worth thinking about."

"I believe," she said, "we ought to go and spend a few days looking around Goldfield and Tonopah. Both horses we got back were found in those towns."

"Probably," I said, "because the varmints who took them suddenly got the wind up and unloaded fast—a little too fast, it might turn out."

She was eyeing me soberly, seriously, I thought. "You mean we might catch sight of some of the others?" Having got back two she seemed to be under a strong compulsion to recover the rest. "All right," I said, "let's do it. But I think we ought to start with Tonopah because if Pers Keach is hooked up with this he might be peddling them locally to get 'em off his hands."

So bright and early next morning we set out for Tonopah. On the way we were hailed by a horsebacker who said, "Aren't you folks from the Pothook?"

When we admitted it he said, "I'm your neighbor on the east, Stan Browdowski. Lazy B. Cows."

We said we were glad to know him. Merrilee invited him to drop by some time and take a look at our outfit. After some more chitchat we shook hands and went on our way, arriving at Tonopah about mid-morning.

Compared with Goldfield I thought it a dinky jerkwater sort of a place, busy enough and obviously thriving, but just about everything built out of wood with the impermanent look of a frontier town. Some of these buildings had false fronts.

We took rooms at White's and rode around getting the hang of this community. Mines and cattle seemed to make it go. "Sort of sprawled out, isn't it?" Merrilee said as we looked around.

I told her I guessed plenty of money changed hands. "People who live around here are a down-to-earth sort, more interested, I'd say, in layin' up treasure than makin' a display; not the kind to care about what others may say of them."

We certainly kept our eyes peeled during the three days we spent there prowling around but we didn't see any of her missing horses. "We're just wastin' our time," I told her. If Horba was there he did a mighty good job of keeping out of our sight. On the fourth day we saddled up and headed for Goldfield.

We did no better there. We saw several of the horses we'd fetched into the country but not any stolen ones. After five days of looking, riding up one street and down another, from the park and school reserves at one end of town to the railroad yards of the Las Vegas & Tonopah depot and north and east to the yards of the Tonopah & Goldfield Rail Road, and a good ways north and west of both lines. We even rode out to the various mines, but not one stolen Rafter horse did we see.

At last, disgruntled with our futile search, Merrilee had had enough of it and said with a wan look at me, "Let's go home."

Back at Pothook we found that McGee had shod all our horses, and a good job he'd made of it. "You git kicked by one now you'll know it," he said with a grunt. "Iron cowboy plates on every last one of 'em." He shoved back his hat and told Merrilee soberly, "Some of these nags ought to be put in training, ma'am."

"They're all halter broke now as you must have discovered." When he nodded she said, "You mean broke to the saddle?"

"That, too, of course. What I mean, ma'am, is you're wastin' a prime source of revenue lettin' these critters stand around gobblin' grass. You got a number of individuals here that could set brush tracks afire an' git you some first-rate advertisin'. I mean some real competitors! You've got good blood and fine conformation an' ort to take advantage of it. You put a few of 'em into match races, ma'am—show what they can do, an' you'll not be able to raise 'em fast enough to satisfy demand."

Merrilee's eyes began to sparkle. "You really think so? You believe that?"

"I know it," McGee said. "I been around horses all my life, and I've yet to see a better bunch than you've got here."

"Can you give them this training?"

"Ma'am," McGee said, "you're lookin at the best horse trainer that ever blew in with the tumbleweeds! You let me pick out five or six to git on with, and inside of three months I guarantee you'll be rakin' in mazuma hand over fist. I'll even venture to say right here this minute you've got at least three that can't be beat."

Before the first month went by—don't ask me how—word got out that we were getting horses ready to match-race all comers, were going to back our bangtails against the world. Folks began coming from miles around to see what was going on. We were finally forced to padlock the gate and keep someone watching with a rifle to see they didn't jump over it.

I began to see a difference in the horses McGee was working with. They were getting legged up and were being fed alfalfa and oats. They carried themselves different and what shone in their eyes was the look of eagles.

He'd taken off their cowboy shoes and had them in racing plates that he'd ordered special through one of the Goldfield stores. Us hands had scraped out a track on a level stretch well away from the fence, and this was where every morning he worked them, lap-and-tap and ask-and-answer ten feet behind a stretched rope that we dropped at his signal. He'd be on one and Benny Crowder on the other, and most of the times it was his horse got there first.

It was plain Nels McGee could palaver in language they understood. Seemed like they'd do anything for him.

One of the things he claimed to be was a foot specialist. The few times I wasn't busy elsewhere I'd hunker alongside him half an hour at a time while he worked with a horse he had taken the shoes off, lifting first one hoof and then another, hefting them in his knowing hand, weighing them, it looked like.

Never hurrying. Sometimes he'd work with a single hoof fifteen or twenty minutes, taking a trifle off here, a fraction off some other place until, finally satisfied, he'd put the new plates back on.

The amazing thing to me was the way they'd stand, sometimes looking down at him, never shifting their weight unless he told them to. You'd almost think they enjoyed having him tinker with them.

"There's a whole lot," he said, "in the way a horse is shod."

Chapter Twenty-Five

"You've sure got the find of a lifetime," I told Merrilee. "Never mind what he costs—give him a half-interest if you have to, but don't let that geezer get away from you."

"He's a marvel, isn't he?"

"We don't know that yet, but if he don't make racehorses out of this bunch I'll be some surprised."

Stovepipe Johnson came back from town in the midst of our discussion. He gave Merrilee an envelope he said was in our box at the post office; we had thought it best not to have rural delivery in case that Tucson bank was still on the hunt for Rafter's foreclosed owner.

It had a pretty important look to it as she stood there turning it over and over with a frown between her eyes. The only writing on it said *Pothook Ranch, Goldfield, Nevada.* No return address. "Who do you suppose could be writing us?" she asked.

Johnson said, "Open it, for cripes' sake, an' let's find out."

"Pretty high-toned paper," I mentioned. "Ain't seen nothin' like it in a coon's age. Go ahead and open it. Stovepipe's all of a lather."

"I don't know," she said, worried like. "Gives me a feeling I can't quite like." She stood there tapping a toe while she stared at it. Seemed as though she'd lost some of her color.

"Give it to Stovepipe. He's not afraid to open it."

So she finally did, and he ripped it open. "Wait a minute," I said. "Where's it from—look at the postmark."

"Says Beatty, Nevada."

"What does that letterhead say?"

"Consumer's Brewing Association. Brewed from the best hops and malts only. Just above that it says Gold Nugget Beer—didn't know they had a plant at Beatty."

"Give it here," she said and, suddenly impatient, grabbed it out of his hand. Her eyes widened. "Listen," she said, kind of hoarse. "Here's what it says. 'Dear Pothook: We would like for you to pick us out ten of your top racing prospects, for which we are prepared to pay twenty-five hundred dollars apiece, delivered here at Beatty stockyards on the twenty-fifth of this month.'"

"Must be some kinda joke," Johnson said. And I said, "Who signed it?"

She looked. "Ira Craig, General Sales Manager. Underneath it says, 'P.S. We are taking the liberty of sending you two kegs of Gold Nugget draft with our compliments.'"

"No check?" Johnson asked.

"Of course there's no check. 'Delivered here at Beatty,' it says."

"Well," I mentioned, "you don't look overjoyed."

"Twenty-five hundred dollars! I can do better than that right here!"

"I wouldn't count on it," Johnson said. "No strings attached, and they're letting you pick them. That's twenty-five thousand bucks in one lump." He looked at me. "Why not show it to McGee?"

"Good idea," I said, and to Merrilee, "Why don't you?"

So we all trooped over to where he was plucking hairs from a sorrel filly's tail. When, looking up, McGee stepped back she handed him the letter. "Tell me what you think of this."

He read it and handed it back. "Seems to be a bona fide offer."

"Could be some kind of hoax," I said.

"A twenty-five-thousand-dollar hoax?" McGee grinned. "Wish somebody would fix up that kinda hoax fer me."

"You think it's all right, then?" Merrilee asked him.

"Says top race prospects, you to pick 'em out. Nothin' said about them bein' developed and ready to run. I'd say for two-year-olds that's a pretty fair price, even for this kind."

She was brightening up considerably, I thought. "But we have to deliver them."

"Not if you don't want to. Tell 'em all transactions are FOB the ranch."

Johnson said, "No return address."

"Seem to be taking a lot for granted," I mentioned.

"Big companies generally do," McGee observed. "At least that's been my experience. Like to throw their weight about. Nothing compelling you to accept their offer. You don't show up with the horses on the specified date, I guess they'll know you're not interested. They want 'em bad enough they might sweeten the kitty."

And Johnson said, "Twenty-five thousand's a pile of cash put right into your hand."

"I don't know," she said, but it was plain she was tempted. "What do you think, Peep? Should I or shouldn't I?"

"They're your horses," I reminded her. "How many two-year-olds have you got?"

"I don't think I have more than ten right now."

"Mull it over a while."

"The twenty-fifth is only eight days from now. It will take at least two to get down there, won't it?"

148

"Nearer three," McGee said, "if you're goin' to keep 'em in good flesh."

She looked from him to me, still trying to make up her mind, I guessed. Thing sounded to me like some kind of con but I kept still, knowing if I came out with this notion it would likely swing her into going ahead with it.

"I'm goin' to town," Stovepipe said and twisted his head for a look at me. "Want to come along?"

He took my grunt for assent, so I was about to get me a horse to fork when Merrilee said, "You've just been there," like she thought it peculiar, and Johnson said, "Forgot somethin'," and got back in the saddle.

"Looked," he said, "like you wasn't much in favor of that ten-horse deal. That's a powerful lot of money for young bangtails that might never run a lick."

"That's the way it struck me," I told him. "Smells fishy— that money's the bait. And it ain't paid yet."

He looked at me like that hadn't occurred to him.

I said, "It's a good piece to Beatty. Us and them horses could run into trouble. Another thing: There's a Gold Nugget brewery right here in town—why go to Beatty?" I kicked it some more. "Why the letter? And what's their sales manager doin' down there?"

"An' no return address," Johnson muttered, thoughtful.

"If it was left to me I'd say ignore it."

"Why didn't you point these things out to her?"

"Because after you kept harpin' on that twenty-five thousand she was just about hooked. Throw cold water on it after what McGee said, she'd just dig in her heels."

Nodding his head and with his wrinkles seeming deeper, Johnson said, "Hear you saw Horba in Tonopah time you discovered that horse of ours at Keach's. You reckon he's back of this?"

"Kind of complicated for him, ain't it?"

"Mebbe we oughta put this up to the sheriff—meant to see him this mornin' but after pickin' up that letter plumb fergot all about it. Aimed to ask if he'd got any line on the rest of them horses."

Sheriff said when we reached him, "We been runnin' around right promiscuous but no, nothing's surfaced. You boys found any more?"

Johnson admitted we'd about given up.

It was just about then this jasper with a led horse in tow pulled up at the hitchrack and, knee round the horn, looked down at us with one of them genial, easy-going smiles. "You the law around here?" he said to Dorn.

"Most of it," the sheriff said, looking him over.

This two-horse galoot, from what he looked like to me, was sort of short and dumpy with a well-padded belly bulging over a hand-tooled belt. Pushed back of his unwrinkled forehead was a dusty black derby and, under it, what's taken for an "open countenance," an unlined skin pulled smooth across its bones and a pair of twinkly eyes about the color of new grass. His mellow voice, just to hear it, was of a kind to inspire confidence.

"Well, neighbor," he announced in the friendliest manner, "my name's Orville Trench and—"

"I reckon," Dorn cut in, "you're here to hunt out some gullibles."

Trench clicked his tongue and let out the smile a couple more notches. "Yep," he chuckled, "that's about the size of it. Pretty near lost my shirt down the road a piece and I'm here to retrench—I make no secret of it. This here critter of mine on the leadshank is open to all comers at a thousand a side."

"Barefoot?" the sheriff asked, peering at the gray's ragged hoofs, tangled mane, and the sleepy eyes in the downhung head.

"Well, yes—can't keep shoes on him. Them sidewalls is

too thin an' brittle. But I'll tell you frankly, shoes on or not, this feller's a sure-enough speed merchant."

"What's the gimmick?" Dorn asked.

"No gimmick. All I got is a heap of faith in this feller's ability, and I'll not deny it sometimes lets me down, like at Beatty. Still, I'm a man of unbounded confidence, Sheriff. I've made my livin' off this ol' skate for nigh on three years."

"What if more'n one fool round here don't share your confidence and wants to have a go at him?"

"Take 'em all on to oncet." He smiled down at Dorn. "No law ag'in' it, is there? I know some place won't stand for gamblin' of any kind."

The sheriff said, "No skin off my nose what they do with their money." He considered Trench a moment. "By your own admission what you're looking for is suckers."

"You bet!" Trench declared. "Horse lovers! Well-heeled gents what'll look at this ol' busted-down pony an' put their dollars where their sense ought to be."

Dorn nodded. "Puttin' it right up front, are you?"

"That's me—honest as the day is long." He ran his twinkly stare over all of us. "I tell 'em straight out I got a world-beater here an' if they don't believe it I'll take them one or a dozen, at a thousand a side. Only one thing I insist on. If there's more than one challenger turns up they've got to all run together. Not even Frisky here is up to runnin' time after time on the same afternoon."

"What's your distance?" Johnson asked.

"Four hundred an' forty yards from a ten-foot score. An' should we get any takers I'd like fer you to be the starter, Sheriff."

"When?" I said.

"Day after tomorrer at four o'clock on a site I'll ask you to pick out," he told Dorn. "You to hold the stakes. That fair enough?"

"We've got a horse we'll run against you," Johnson declared.

"Fine," Trench said.

"You want a look at her?"

"Don't care what any of 'em look like long's their owners can put up the price."

"One thing you better keep in mind," the sheriff mentioned. "Fair warning, Trench. I catch you runnin' in a ringer or any other sort of sleight-of-hand shenanigan, you get free board till I'm fed up with lookin' at you. After that you get rode out on a rail."

Chapter Twenty-Six

"What do you think?" Johnson asked as we headed for home.

"I think you stuck your neck out. That crummy-lookin' gray is going to make a lot of folks look sick. You notice Trench's only thought is to make sure the competitors can scrape up the price; that's why Dorn is picked to hold the stakes. For the distance, that gray is probably a streak of greased lightning."

"Well, accordin' to McGee we got some lightnin' ourselfs. Hell, you could see every rib that nag has got!"

"Don't mean a thing. Some of these sprinters hit their fastest lick when they look half-starved."

"Well . . . we got to find out what McGee's worth to us, ain't we? Keepin' him on the payroll's costin' us a heap, an' if these bangtails of Merrilee's just haven't got it it's time we found out."

I grinned. "You probably ought to tell her that."

"By gollies, Peep, I'm a-goin' to. I ain't knockin' our horses—they're a fine-lookin' bunch, but pretty is as pretty does. Her old man never would race, and I figure it's time we found out!' "

"I reckon we will if she puts one of them up against that gray."

"Where's your faith, man?"

"Right where it's always been, locked up in my pocket. Fellers that make their livin' like Trench, bangin' around from pillar to post with what you'd call a beat-up old skate, are not dang fools or they wouldn't be doing it."

"We'll see," Stovepipe growled. "I wasn't born yestiday!"

"You ought to've told that to Plaza."

"That son of a bitch!" Johnson snarled. "Just let me git my hands on that feller—I'll wring him drier'n a last year's leaf!"

Wasn't much more to say after that. When we got off our mounts in the Pothook yard and Stovepipe took out for the house at his rolling gait I tagged along to see how she'd take it.

After explaining to her about this Trench and what the man had said about his decrepit-looking nag and his challenge to all comers, he admitted he'd engaged on behalf of Pothook to run a horse against him.

"Why certainly—of course we will! I've been eating my heart out for a public chance to show what they can do. How much did you say we have to put up?"

Johnson looked a mite nervous, I thought, watching him. Merrilee, too, kind of gulped at the price. Not that she couldn't afford it these days. It was just that she had this thing about money. Came, no doubt, from those tough times back at Rafter. But she straightened out her face and, nodding, said, "Fine. Day after tomorrow? Four o'clock, you said? Why so late in the day, I wonder?"

"Nothin' strange about that," I told her. "After he puts half of Goldfield in hock he won't want to linger where he'll make a good target."

She gave me a look. "I suppose that's some of your south-of-the-border humor," she sniffed. "Let's go chin with Nels McGee."

We found him, as usual, fooling around with those six he'd picked out for training. Merrilee gave him the gist of the situation. "Is that all right with you?" she asked with unusual humility.

McGee pushed it around through his mind for a while. "The three months I'd counted on ain't up yet," he said, staring at the filly he'd just been currying. Still with the brush in hand, he said, "What did you think of that feller's horse, Peep?"

"Way he looks now," I said, "and how he'll look when he gets into that race is apt to be some different. Tell you the truth, he didn't honestly look like he could make it to the barn. But them's the kind you got to watch out for."

Our horse expert nodded. "True. Stud horse or gelding?"

"Gelded."

"Hmmm. How old would you say?"

"Kept his mouth closed. At a guess I'd say long five or six."

"What's his pasterns look like?"

"Stands up pretty well on them."

McGee gave another sort of tentative nod. He said to Merrilee, "This here three-year-old might not shame us too bad."

We all eyed the filly, short on top with a long underline. Good chest and legs, good quarters. Bright and inquiring eye.

McGee said, "How much you got to put up to start her?"

When told the price McGee looked sober. "Mmmm. Slick customer. Doesn't want to scare out the small fry. Wants to catch enough of 'em to make it worth while."

Johnson said with an incredulous look, "You sound like that's cheap."

"As these things go, dirt cheap. Fellers like Trench are mostly out to git top dollar. Lot of 'em wouldn't bother with less than ten grand."

"He's set the time," I said, at four in the evenin'. Gold-field. Day after tomorrow. Sheriff to hold the stakes and serve as starter. Four-forty. Behind a rope with a ten-foot score. Any of that bother you?"

McGee showed a smile. "No," he said, "I can't say it does. Don't reckon you ever put a name to this here sorrel, ma'am?"

Merrilee shook her head.

"Well," he said, "for her entrance into high society—you might say her deboo on the leaky roof circuit—let's call her Pothook. Might's well git somethin' going fer the others—word o' mouth, I mean."

Next day, along about the middle of it, Nels McGee decided to meander into town. He didn't say why but he came back full of news. This fellow Trench had taken a room at the Esmeralda Hotel and had left that poor old horse of his tied up to the hotel hitchrack for most all day right out in the sun, giving him no attention at all. Last night for supper he'd been given a few corn shucks. For breakfast this morning Trench had thrown down another handful. Folks who had told McGee about this thought it a crying shame. A delegation had approached Sheriff Dorn about the matter but had been shrugged off. "His horse," Dorn said. "No business of ours."

News of the upcoming race had spread like a brush fire, McGee told Merrilee. For miles around folks were piling into town, by spring wagon and surrey, buckboard and horseback and even afoot. Up to the time he'd left, he said, four other horses had come up to scratch in addition to Pothook, making the projected go a six-horse race. Excitement was rampant.

It was to take place on a fairly level stretch of the Park Reserve near the edge of town. Dorn had stepped off the course, and one of his deputies with a bucket of whitewash had marked out both start and finish lines. A good many bets had already been laid, and it was said Orville Trench was accepting all wagers, betting two for one on his horse Frisky. Tomorrow had every earmark of becoming an historic occasion in the history of Goldfield, a day to mark time by. But Trench wasn't having things all his own way; a number of the more cagey gamblers had given Frisky the once-over and were putting their money on him hand over fist.

Two kegs of Gold Nugget draft were delivered from the local brewery, and one of these set up under Merrilee's admonishing eye with instructions to indulge lightly; the proper time to celebrate being after the event. How much attention was bestowed on such notions was, I thought, debatable.

The day of the Big Go dawned bright and clear.

Pothook, McGee declared, was about as ready as she ever would be. Nothing had been decreed about weight and riders, so McGee, with a deal of advice, was putting little Benny Crowder up.

Time began to turn as slow as cold sorghum, but eventually the outfit, with the sole exception of Dry Creek Folsom, set out for the great occasion, Folsom having agreed to stay behind and tend the store with Merrilee's permission to hit that keg for all he could hold.

We arrived in town with an hour to kill. All the other entrants were already on tap and, save for Frisky, were being walked around either by their owners or the persons designated as jockeys. Frisky, it was said, was still tied up at the hotel hitchrack. "That feller's a fool," one of the other owners said. "He treats that nag like a bucket of slops." I walked about with Merrilee to discover what the competition looked like.

Three of the four were big, chunky, fine-looking animals that, in the midst of her exclamations, I said would do first rate in a horse show, probably take all the ribbons. The fourth one looked like a cart mare and this one I eyed with some trepidation. Her owner, a gaunt and dried-up-looking old harridan in patched overalls, gave me a knowing grin. This appeared to vex Merrilee, who said as soon as we got out of earshot, "What was she grinning at you for?" and I said, "Can't imagine—never saw her before in my life."

Which was true enough, but I had her pegged for another who'd come out of the same mold as Trench.

Time we got back to the starting place we couldn't get near it for the onlookers packed ten and twelve deep and, back of them, a great clutter of buggies and wagons and even in these a lot of folks were standing. "Let's go down along the side here," I muttered. "If we stay on our mounts maybe we can see over them hats and bonnets—never saw such a mob!"

They'd have been all over the space allotted to the runners except for the batch of special deputies Dorn had sworn in to hold them back. And behind the finish line another great crush was gathered, jammed elbow to elbow save for a narrow lane left for the horses.

Merrilee was pretty excited, jabbering away forty words to the second.

Dorn, we could see, had finally got the horses lined up behind the stretched rope a pair of star-packers were hanging onto. Three of those entries were excited as Merrilee and kept edging forward one after another until Dorn looked about to call the whole thing off.

He didn't, of course. He finally put the hand with the pistol over his head. Like the veteran he was, Trench's horse stood still as a rock with the others jiggling and sidling along either side of him.

Dorn's pistol barked, the rope was dropped, and Merrilee gasped as Pothook went up on her hind legs pawing the air with the rest of the field getting two lengths ahead of her. Merrilee groaned. "She'll never make it!" A whole bevy of groans accompanied hers, with a liberal sprinkling of cusswords. Benny hammered our filly down on all fours, and then she got busy, overhauling in six jumps the three that had looked like show horses. But that woebegone Frisky had opened up a lead it seemed impossible to overcome, his nearest competitor being that old harridan's cart mare three lengths back.

Merrilee suddenly was yelling like a fiend. *"Pothook! Pothook—go it, Pothook!"* And Pothook was certainly making a move, edging up on the cart mare jump by jump. Others now were taking up the chant. Trench, on the gray, twisted his head for a look but apparently saw no cause for worry with his gray still a good two lengths in the lead and the whitewashed finish line not a hundred yards ahead.

Benny, equipped like the rest, wasn't using his bat. Crouched well forward above her stretched-out neck, I thought it looked like he was talking to her, and the game filly responded. Passing the old woman's mare she began creeping up on the flying Frisky.

Now she had her head past his quarters. Now it was up to his shoulders. You could see Benny with his mouth to her ear again and now they were sprinting neck and neck and the finish line scarcely fifty feet away.

The crowd was going wild. *"Pothook! Pothook!"* they were crying over and over, some of them jumping up and down. Even those without any money at stake didn't want no rank outsider taking this. *"Pothook! Pothook!"* they yelled in a frenzy, and now she had her nose out in front. Two more jumps took them over the line, and it was Pothook the victor by a short head!

Chapter Twenty-Seven

Merrilee, leaning out from her saddle, flung both arms around me and in her excitement kissed me smack on the mouth. "Oh, Peep!" she cried. "Isn't it wonderful!"

"How much did you have on her?"

"Not a penny!" she gasped. "But wasn't it *great*? I honestly didn't think she could do it—and after that horrible start! When that pistol was fired and she went into the air I thought we were finished."

I nodded. "Takes a mighty fine nag in a four-forty race to overcome that kind of handicap. That race was billed as a winner-take-all; Pothook's earned you five thousand smackeroos. Guess you'll have to jump her sellin' price up some."

"You think I'd part with her after that? She's got a home with me as long as she lives!"

A lot of the folks, I noticed, were looking just as gleeful as she was; you could pick out winners by the looks on their faces. Trench came up to us leading his gray. "Well," he said, "congratulations, Miz Manton. That's some filly—and she won fair an' square. Going by the way she reared up at the start I'd guess you haven't really raced her much."

"That was her first race," Merrilee declared, eyes bright as diamonds.

He shook his head. "You got a right to feel proud. Haven't very many critters beat this old horse." Touching his hat he went off with the gray, walking him around to get him cooled out.

Benny and McGee came up then with Pothook. McGee had thrown a blanket over her. He put the reins in Benny's hands and told him to walk her up to the Union Feed Stables, then rub her down good, and put her in a stall. And stay with her. "Better let him have your gun, Peep, just in case some highbinder tries to make off with her."

"You stayin' over?" I asked.

"Figure I better. I'll keep Benny with me, and we'll come home in the cool of the mornin'."

As McGee went off to pick up his own horse, the sheriff called out to us over the heads of the departing crowd. We rode over to where he was standing, and he put a fat roll of bills into Merrilee's hand. "Here's your winnings," he grinned. "Looks like you're breedin' the right kind. Reckon your business will pick up right smart after that demonstration."

Quite a few of the crowd had pushed up to congratulate her, and one of them, a well-dressed dude in a stovepipe hat, said if she had another like the one he'd just watched he was in a prime mood to buy. "Fact," he said, "if you're of a mind to sell her I'll pay whatever price you want to put on her."

She thanked him nicely but said she guessed not.

I finally got her headed for home.

Soon as McGee and Benny Crowder showed up with Pothook next morning, she told McGee he'd be wanted at the house as quick as he was free. She told me to find Johnson and fetch him, too.

When, like a schoolmarm, she finally had us in front of her, she said, "I've decided to accept that order from Beatty. We'll be leaving here day after tomorrow. Early as possible." With her glance sweeping over us, she asked, "Any comments?"

When nobody spoke she waved us away.

Outside I told Johnson, "I'm goin' to town. Be back before noon. Okay?"

"Go ahead."

First thing I did on reaching Goldfield was hunt up the brewery, which turned out to be at 243 Brewery Street, not far from where yesterday's race had been held. I'd had plenty of time on the way in to get my thoughts in order.

Ever since she'd got that letter I'd been suspicious of this deal. It had seemed to me that anyone prepared to spend that much money in one lump for ten young horses would be bound to include a return address. The object, obviously, was to put those horses on the road where they could be got at. And having glimpsed Horba in Tonopah I had thought it plumb likely he'd be in this thing someplace. It had been like a crushing weight hanging over us suspended by the slenderest of threads.

Also it had seemed to me this was part and parcel of the same weasily mind which had planned that cut-fence snatch. There was bound, I thought, to be several ideal places between here and Beatty that would be first rate for setting up an ambush. The fellow engineering this wanted these horses and had no intention of paying for them. That twenty-five thousand was the bait he'd dangled that, to me, suggested more than a speaking acquaintance with Merrilee. And the reason I hadn't protested more strongly was the notion I'd got that here was probably the best chance we'd get for sure enough putting these rogues out of business.

I hated to risk Merrilee's horses but I felt like without them we'd never lay eyes on those buggers. And there was certainly someone smarter than Horba at the head of this hoax. That was the jasper we needed to eliminate.

This trip to the brewery was undertaken simply to confirm what I figured was cooking.

In the brewery's office a man left his desk to ask what could be done for me.

I said, "I'm from the Pothook ranch. Couple days ago you people sent us two kegs of draft beer without charge. I'd like to know and thank whoever was responsible."

"I'll look up the order." Back at his desk he opened a thick ledger.

"Apparently," he said, after riffling a few pages, "the order and the cash for it was left on my desk, so I've no idea who this customer could be."

"We had a letter from Beatty saying we'd be getting this beer with the brewery's compliments."

"We have no plant at Beatty."

"The letter was signed by Ira Craig, who professed to be your general sales manager."

"Yes," he nodded, "that's Mr. Craig's title, but he's on vacation someplace in Idaho."

I said to his rather puzzled look, "Thanks a lot," and took my departure.

Way it looked to me, Dirk Horba or some other underling had sneaked in there some noon when the staff was off to lunch and helped himself to a piece of their stationery. Horba wasn't very bright but if he had swiped the letterhead you'd have thought he'd have been instructed to get an official envelope for it. But no, probably not since they'd been careful not to furnish an address we could write to. This was to be a take-it-or-leave-it proposition with the dangled bait of that twenty-five thousand figure to push Merrilee into doing what they wanted.

All we had to do now was make sure the jaws of this trap closed on somebody else.

When I got back to the ranch I got Stovepipe aside and told him what I'd discovered. "I'm pretty near sure this is the same outfit that cut our fence, so we can leave Benny here to tend the store while the rest of us head for Beatty with the ten ordered horses. Two of us, I think, will be enough to fetch those nags into what I'm sure will be an ambush. I'm not trying to take over your job as top screw but I reckon you're as anxious as I am to nail these rascals, and I've a notion I know how to do it."

"Go right ahead," Stovepipe said.

"Well, I don't figure they'll be a heap anxious to shoot Merrilee if shootin's what they've got in mind, so she and Dry Creek could handle the horses, which leaves you, me, and McGee to clear up this business and put those devils where they belong.

"I'm for that," Johnson said. "But how're we gonna do it?"

"That's what I'm working on now. They'll probably have some small fry watching to make sure we've bit. So we'll all go along for ten miles or so. At about that point we'll leave Merrilee and Dry Creek with the horses. The rest of us will quit the road and push on ahead and find out where they've set up their trap. Okay?"

"You bet—sounds like a winner!"

Next time I had a chance to talk with McGee, I asked if he could handle a rifle. He said he could so I explained what we had in mind. McGee nodded. "All right with me, but I think you ought to get the sheriff to go along. That way if someone gets rubbed out we'll have the law on our side."

Next morning I told Johnson what McGee had said, and he took off for town to take care of it. He had just got back when a fellow in city clothes rode into the yard with a sharp look at Stovepipe before he said, "Howdy. I'm hunting the Pothook outfit."

"You've come to the right place," Stovepipe assured him. "Git down an' rest your saddle."

"Your name Johnson?" the man said as he stepped out of the saddle. He was a tall lean jasper with a hard pair of eyes above a long nose and a gimlet mouth. When Stovepipe said his name was Johnson, this fellow said, "Taken me quite a spell to run you people down; without the help of Western Union I might never have done it. My name's O'Hara, special investigator for the Beach and Bascomb bank at Tucson."

Chapter Twenty-Eight

You can imagine the jolt that gave us.

Stovepipe stared, speechless. Not reckoning he'd be foolish enough to reach for his pistol, just in case I hastened to say, "Guess you're here about those horses we didn't leave behind when we moved?"

"Among other things." His grin was on the sardonic side. "You got a place in the shade where we can talk this out?"

Johnson allowed we could probably find one and led us over to the bunkhouse porch. I guessed it was his intention to keep this fellow away from Merrilee long as he could. "Who," asked O'Hara, "is the owner of this property?"

Johnson let out a sigh. "Merrilee Manton. Reckon you already know that."

"She prepared to reimburse the bank for the horses she absconded with?"

"Expect that'll depend on what value the bank puts on them."

"There is also the matter," the bank's agent said, "of two stallions and the fourteen mares the Gourd and Vine lost."

I said, "We understood Manton had paid for those horses."

"Well, he didn't."

Johnson said, "If you go over his accounts you'll see where he drew out the money for those horses."

The man exhibited another chilly smile.

"Can't see," I said, "how the Gourd and Vine horses come into this, or how they concern you, O'Hara."

"I've been asked to look into it."

"Manton's dead. Been buried three years. Guess you'll just have to forget that part of it."

That got me a long hard look. "And how do *you* come into this?"

"Let's just say I'm a friend of the family."

"Indeed," he said with another wintry look. "Unless you want to see this whole outfit charged with taking horses out of Arizona that belonged to the Beach and Bascomb bank—"

"Just a minute," I said. "When those horses left Arizona they belonged to Merrilee Manton. The bank at that time hadn't foreclosed. Let's just keep the record straight. What value has your client put on those horses—and I'm speaking of the horses that left Rafter. Not necessarily what you see here."

He considered me a while and finally said, "Five hundred dollars apiece. In round figures the bank expects to be paid thirty thousand dollars unless Manton's daughter wants to find herself in court."

Johnson said, "Guess you're forgetting this here is Nevada."

"Yes," I said, "you're a considerable distance from where you claim—"

"Are you or aren't you going to pay for those horses?"

"The two stallions were left at the ranch, they weren't taken," Johnson said. "If I was to hand you a certified check for twenty-five thousand, will you, as the bank's agent—"

"As the bank's representative," O'Hara said, "I'll want first to see that check on the table. Did you know this 'friend of the family' graduated from Yale and owns a cow spread near Brady, Texas?"

Stovepipe's eyes wheeled in my direction, a pair of windows with the shades pulled down.

Seemed like O'Hara had spent a considerable portion of his time on homework. A formidable antagonist but not, I hoped, an irrepressible one. "So what?" I said. "No law against it." Seemed to me this was the time to put him into the picture from Merrilee's side of the coin.

So I mentioned the various troubles we'd been having, the losses she'd taken in getting here, the Paiutes who'd chased us into Death Valley, the fence-cutting episode, the desertions and killings—

"You're making me cry," O'Hara cut in with curled lip. "I notice you haven't mentioned the sales and the money she picked up from that horse race."

Ignoring this jab I mentioned the letter we'd got from Beatty with its spurious offer of twenty-five thousand for ten sprinting prospects and what we proposed to do about it. "If you're concerned about our sales I suggest you come along in your role of bank's agent and help us put the finger on some *real* horse thieves."

"I most certainly will. An outfit wily as this one could be setting up another hoax to defraud the bank of its legal property!"

Hearing the approach of Merrilee's step I grinned at him nastily. "And as the Beach and Bascomb bank's representative, you'll want, I expect, to be one of those who accompany the horses?"

"That's exactly right," O'Hara said, taking off his hat. "And this, I suppose, is the elusive Merrilee Manton."

"Who is this man?" she said from white cheeks.

"A bill collector that Tucson bank has sent up here hunting for Rafter horses," I said, "hoping to squeeze thirty thousand out of you."

I saw the frantic look in her glance and the ugly look on the range dick's mouth. "Name's O'Hara. He's goin' to help you and Dry Creek get those horses down to Beatty."

With Benny Crowder left at Pothook, the rest of us set out early next morning armed with rifles on the long trek to Beatty. There was very little conversation. The two-year-olds were fresh and eager, our biggest job being to hold them down and keep them in as good flesh as possible. And it *was* quite a job those first couple of miles, after which they settled down nicely.

It was a warm and sultry morning with all the earmarks of becoming a scorcher once the sun burned away that low drift of clouds. I could not read any key to his thoughts on Stovepipe's rugged countenance but worry was plain in Merrilee's frown. If any watcher had taken note of our departure he had managed to keep himself out of sight and by this time had probably sent off his wire. This was what I was counting on to mobilize the horse thieves.

After we'd gone about ten miles into the desert and left the hummocks and hills well behind, Johnson, McGee, and myself cut away from the horse handlers, and at an increased gait rode off on a tangent designed to disassociate ourselves from the main party.

Johnson asked, "What are we goin' to do about that bastard O'Hara?"

"I expect he'll come around. Though it might not be a bad thing," I said, "if we could come to some agreement on what she owes the bank and persuade her to pay it."

"There's goin' to be some more hills and considerable brush farther on as I remember this route," McGee mentioned. "Might not be as easy as you think to locate those rascals."

"There's only a couple places really that would serve their purpose," Johnson said through his scowl. "We'll know when we get there. Let's shake it up a little."

We put our mounts into an easy lope for about half an hour to make sure we were far enough ahead of the others to scout around a bit in case the ambush wasn't where Stovepipe figured it would be. After which we dropped once more into a walk, no one seeming to have much to say.

The morning wore on, the heat increasing as the sun got higher.

"We goin' to try and take those buggers alive?" McGee wanted to know.

"Probably be better if we can," I said. "A public hanging might serve as a discouragement to others of their kind. It will depend, I suppose, on the way things shape up. If there's goin' to be fireworks, let them start it."

Nels McGee nodded.

When we presently saw the low blue hills in the distance begin to assume their natural color he said, "Off there is where the sheriff aimed to join us. Let's hope he hasn't forgotten to show up."

"Seems a pretty conscientious sort," I said.

When we came within gunshot of the hills a horsebacker waving his hat abruptly showed above the sage. "Looks like him," Johnson said.

Dorn came forward to meet us. "You guessed right," he said to me after greetings were exchanged. "Those rascals are in position about two miles west of here where the road curls through these hummocks—six of them just this side of the road. I came down here last night where I'd be in time to see their approach. They settled in about an hour ago so I came back to be sure you didn't blunder into them. It ain't enough to know what they're up to. What we want is to catch them at it."

McGee said, "How do you want to handle this? You figure on taking them back for trial?"

"Round here," Dorn said with his brows up, "we don't try thieves, we eliminate them."

"I imagine," I told him, "we've got about an hour before those horses reach the ambush."

Johnson, still frowning, said, "How far south of here?"

"About a mile and two miles west."

"Ain't the place I reckoned they'd pick," Stovepipe said.

Dorn said, "That's where I saw them. They was off their horses rollin' up smokes."

Johnson shrugged. "Reckon I guessed wrong. Recognize any of them?"

"Didn't git close enough. Vermin's vermin whatever tag you put on 'em."

Johnson spat out a mouthful of tobacco leaves and gnawed a fresh chew off a battered-looking plug. "Hadn't we better sort of mosey on?"

"No hurry," the sheriff said. "I want to catch them villains in the process."

"Miz Manton's with those horses."

"Molestin' a woman'll git you hanged quicker'n anything."

So we poked along, keeping our ears skinned, sort of drifting in a southwesterly direction, Johnson still scowling and muttering under his breath. Dorn, twisting around in his saddle, finally said in an exasperated tone, "If you're so sure you're right, take off," and Stovepipe, brightening, turned his mount and pointed his horse straight into the west.

I looked at the sheriff. "You don't think he's right?"

"Damn it," Dorn said, "I saw 'em, didn't I? Hunkered around, starin' down at the road like they was figurin' to wait all day if they had to."

When some twenty minutes later we came in sight of the place, Dorn ripped out an oath, and I felt a cold shiver run up my back. Dorn drove his horse at a brushy slope, and I was hard on his heels, McGee tagging after me. "Right there," Dorn said, pointing. "You can see their boot marks plain as paint."

No two ways about that. But they weren't there now.

We wheeled our animals and headed north. And had hardly got started when the crack-crack of rifle fire came down on the wind, and we kicked our mounts into a hard run.

We were down on the road when five minutes later McGee yelled, "Look!"

But already I'd seen the Pothook two-year-olds streaking off every whichway like splattering grease from a too-hot skillet, and beyond and back of them a mad scramble of gyrating horsebackers blasting away at each other with rifles.

Too much dust and way too much movement to know friend from foe. Not till we were practically onto them did the villains discover us and, in a flurry of wheeling, four ridden ponies abruptly tore from the melee and went larruping off, spurred, reins slashing, in a desperate bid to get into the hills.

Dorn's rifle came up. I saw him squeeze trigger, and the hindmost rider with flailing arms went sideways off his careening horse as the others slammed round the hill out of sight.

Scarcely two rods behind we went into the turn full tilt, geehawed round that spur of the hill and straight into the muzzles of flame-wreathed rifles. In that bedlam of sound McGee went off the back of his horse with mouth wide open. Dorn's horse stumbled and went down in a heap as mine sailed over a crouched shape, one hind hoof smashing the lifted head like an eggshell. One sidelong glimpse I caught of Plaza, and the ground rushed up as the horse dropped from under me.

Chapter Twenty-Nine

Well, as Dorn had said, we don't fool around with thieves in Nevada.

Time I'd got enough breath to pick myself up, the whole thing was over, the sheriff swearing over the loss of his pony, standing there hatless a rope's length away.

Peering round half-dazed from the spill I had taken I saw McGee on one knee trying to staunch the blood leaking out of a shoulder. "See if you can get him patched up," Dorn growled and, scooping up his hat, went off round the bend to see to those of our party who had been with the horses, which were probably scattered to hell and gone.

I had no recollection of firing a shot but there was not left alive even one of the crouched villains who'd so nearly helped us out of this world. "Damn slug's still in there," McGee muttered as I came up to him.

I put a clean folded handkerchief against the hole and bound it in place with strips torn from his shirttail. "Guess that'll have to do," I said, "till we can get you to Goldfield."

I remembered then the fleeting glimpse I'd had of Fenton's face with those rifles spitting at us and walked back to take a look. And sure enough there he was, our bogus Plaza dead as a doornail where a slug had caught him square in the throat.

Reckon I should have guessed a lot sooner who'd been back of the tribulations we'd been through, for he wasn't the kind to quit at a setback. Well, he'd got one now he couldn't crawl out of, and I guessed we might have some peace at last. If we could manage to deal with that damned O'Hara.

I followed McGee down the slope to the huddle of shapes swapping talk with the sheriff, and heard Merrilee say, "First order of business is to come up with my horses!"

Sounded like she was in fine fettle, and the realization came over me—and some guilt along with it—I'd been too taken up in that fight to do any proper worrying about her. Should have known, of course, from the very start that Merrilee Manton was an obvious survivor.

As I came up with the group I noticed Dry Creek with a bandaged forearm and Stovepipe Johnson with a stained rag showing below his chin-strapped hat. "Where's O'Hara?" I said looking round, not seeing him.

"Must of leaned ag'in' a bullet," Dry Creek offered. "You'll find him off there with them two varmints we dropped," and stuck out his good arm to point out the direction. "One of 'em's Dirk Horba, an' good riddance, I say."

Eyeing McGee and the handiwork I'd done on him she said, "Hadn't we better get those horses caught up and be on our way?"

"Yes," I said, "Nels here's got a slug ought to be taken out," and ran my look across Johnson's unrevealing face. We put McGee on a horse with Dry Creek to look after him and told them to get going.

Took the rest of us something more than an hour to round up those two-year-olds and the two bandits' horses that had come through the fracas in still usable shape.

The sheriff led off with Stovepipe alongside of him, then Merrilee's young sprinters—docile enough now, with her and myself bringing up the rear. She presently said after a searching look at me, "You don't look too perky yourself."

"Took a spill," I said. "Nothin' broken, just bruised a mite where I scuffed up the ground. Lot of shale on that hillside."

She didn't look as concerned as she might have, I thought. I reckoned her mind was still on those horses. But I was wrong about that, for she said sort of tentative, "I dislike sounding callous, but don't you think it might be—all things considered—rather comfortable for us that fellow O'Hara happened, as Dry Creek said, to have leaned against a bullet?"

"Yeah," I said dryly. "Rather fortunate, I'd call it. Johnson gets to stay on the payroll, and you can keep the thirty thousand O'Hara sort of mentioned as the least he'd take to get off our backs."

"But the horses were mine when we quit Rafter—the bank hadn't foreclosed. He hadn't a leg to stand on!"

"Well, that's one way of lookin' at it."

"It's the right way. You know very well I'm no horse thief!"

"Of course not. No court in the land could look at you and ever believe it."

Her glance skewered me suspiciously. I gave her a grin and said, "I'm serious."

"Oh, Peep . . . I never know when you're putting me on—or off, for that matter. Do you think Stovepipe shot O'Hara?"

Looking straight ahead, I said, "What would he want to do a thing like that for?"

"Well, he might have thought he'd be saving me some money."

"Wouldn't that be carryin' his obligation just a mite beyond the call of duty?" I gave her another grin and said, "Let's talk about ourselves for a change. You still of the same mind about gettin' hitched?"

"Now what's brought that up?" She eyed me obliquely. "You know, Peep, you can sometimes say the damndest things."

"You denyin' you said you hadn't laid eyes on a man you'd be satisfied to spend the rest of your life with?"

A bit of extra color came into her cheeks. "Some things I don't like to joke about."

"Hell, I'm not jokin'."

"Let's be serious, Peep. Is this a proposition or are you honestly suggesting I marry you?"

"Of course I am. Told you that back at Rafter. Merrilee Boyano—try it on for size. Ain't that got a dreamy sound?"

"Oh, Peep!" Impulsive as always, she pretty near pulled me off my horse.